Aesop's Fox

A Mobtown Tale of a Boy and The Great Fire

Aesop's Fox

John Thomas Everett

Aura Libertatis Spirat

AESOP'S FOX

Braveship Books
www.braveshipbooks.com
Aura Libertatis Spirat

Cover Design by Rossitsa Atanassova

Book layout by Alexandru Diaconescu
www.steadfast-typesetting.eu

ISBN-13: 978-1-64062-200-5
Printed and bound in the United States of America

Contents

Acknowledgments

Aesop's Fox is the third novel of my Baltimore trilogy and as much as I love the city, my plan is to leave it behind for a while. Before I do, however, I must acknowledge its rich and fascinating history and thank the city for getting me started writing in the first place. I would not be surprised if at some future point the place drew me back.

This last of the three Baltimore books has taken me a bit longer to complete because I was becalmed by a lack of direction for my characters. I had a story to tell but no one to tell it. I just couldn't rouse them enough to show me which way to go. In earlier efforts, my players seemed to forge their own way and all I had to do was be faithful to them in the words I chose. I got no such guidance in *Aesop's Fox*, at first. If it wasn't for my wife, Marge, prodding me gently but persistently, I might still be jumping and missing beautifully ripe, sweet grapes and calling them bitter. One more leap got me restarted and the novel's characters began to talk to me again. So, I'd like to say thanks one more time to my true-blue partner for helping me take that last leap.

Somewhere in the back of my head there's a voice saying: real novelists' acknowledgments are of serious literary figures or professionals who spend their lives working with writers. I have ignored that voice since my exposure to such giants is, shall we say, minimal. I also have ignored it because I am blessed with family and friends whose opinions I respect and whose help I trust. Time and again, they have come through with valuable suggestions, tweaks, doses of reality, and no fear in telling me something doesn't work. While this feedback sometimes comes in answer to a cryptic question I've asked, or an incongruous conversation I've started, it also arrives directly as a result of the work of wading through various iterations of my manuscripts. Of these stalwarts, I like to say (again) thanks to my brothers Chris and Tim Everett, my sister Kate Warr, my daughter Emily Hunyadi, and my true and long-time buds, Mike Lent and Paul Mueller.

Hopefully, the sources listed in Appendix II adequately capture the many places and people I've drawn upon to tell my story with historical accuracy and sufficient depth to interest and gain the reader's trust. Among these, I'd like to acknowledge with some emphasis: The Maryland Center for History and Culture (until recently, The Maryland Historical Society), the historical archives of *The Baltimore Sun*, The Enoch Pratt Central Library, The US Department of the Interior National Parks Service, and the C&O Canal National Historical Park in Cumberland, Maryland.

Finally, I'd like to recognize those who have assisted me in getting *Aesop's Fox* into print. The fine work of Kimberly Hunt, a superb editor with the Baltimore Company, Revision Division (www.revisiondivision.com), turned my grammarian's nightmare into a readable whole. And, of course, I'd like to thank, Jeff Edwards, eminent author of military thrillers and the heart and soul of Braveship Books, for his shepherding me through the publishing labyrinth once again.

The Fox & the Grapes

A Fox one day spied a beautiful bunch of ripe grapes hanging from a vine trained along the branches of a tree. The grapes seemed ready to burst with juice, and the Fox's mouth watered as he gazed longingly at them.

The bunch hung from a high branch, and the Fox had to jump for it. The first time he jumped he missed it by a long way. So he walked off a short distance and took a running leap at it, only to fall short once more. Again and again he tried, but in vain.

Now he sat down and looked at the grapes in disgust.

"What a fool I am," he said. "Here I am wearing myself out to get a bunch of sour grapes that are not worth gaping for."

And off he walked very, very scornfully.

—Aesop's Fables; Aesop c.620 BCE – 564 BCE

"...If you can dream - and not make dreams your master..."

—from *If...* by Rudyard Kipling, 1895

Part I

Western Maryland

CHAPTER 1

THE FOXES

The boy's father was a big man and often miscalculated the power of his punch, especially when he had been into the corn. So, Ruddie had learned how to be as invisible as possible, when to stay still, and when to bolt for cover. He could almost smell trouble coming.

Sharecropping on someone else's patch of rocks and stumps was a hard life and it made a man hard, both inside and out. So hard, in fact, that the man the locals called "Big Russ" frequently sought relief from it. That usually meant getting drunk and finding something to hit. Sometimes it was one of the men from the village of Mt. Savage, sometimes it was one of the blacks from the farm a mile down the road, and sometimes it was Ruddie's mother. At least it was, until she died two years ago from what the boy assumed was heartbreak and disappointment.

It was already 1898 when the Quick family quit the streets and alleys of Baltimore for the work that was offered in the Eckhart Coal Mines at the base of Big Savage Mountain in western Maryland. It wasn't long after, however, that Big Russ' drinking got him fired from the mines. Since neither the iron works or the rail yards in the area would hire him, Russ Quick fell to the lowest economic rung as a tenant farmer on land only worked by ex-slaves and poor white trash—the name Ruddie had heard some boys call him.

Off and on he would ask his mother why they lived where they did, away from people and other things. The first time he asked, he watched her look quickly at his father, then turn away at his glare. All she said after that was, "To find some peace." But that was four years ago and no peace he had ever heard of had yet been found.

When he and his mother were alone and he pressed her on their life in the city, she had little to say. The most he could get her to tell him was that Big Russ had been a fireman. Once, after a particularly unfair whipping, enfolded in his mother's arms, he asked why she even married Big Russ. Her answer was slow in coming and faltering when it came. With great effort she told him that she had been very poor and about to have a baby. Ruddie didn't really understand that but sensed asking more about it would cause his mother pain.

He was six at the time they moved up to Allegany County from Baltimore and Ruddie remembered little about the city they left behind, except that he was scared and hungry most of the time. Just like now. In earlier days, they had a family: his mother, his father, his sister, Nora, and him. But, Nora, his only friend, had died of consumption a year after arriving on the farm. She was buried up on the ridge under a tulip poplar and a wooden cross made of slats from the shed the wind blew down. His mother had written on the marker: "Our dearest Nora, gone to her reward."

Ruddie hoped that his sister had gotten her reward because he loved her and she loved him. He knew it because it was Nora he went to after a beating when his father would threaten his mother not to "coddle the boy." His sister would hold him until he stopped crying, sing softly to him and stroke his hair.

Ruddie often thought about Nora's reward, mainly about what his own reward would be and whether it was worth dying for. He was forced to think about his own existence, even as young as he was, by the fact of his angry father. There were times when, hiding in his special place, he would fight back the tears while trying to ignore the pain caused by a balled fist or a piece of knotted rope or something else at hand. It was then that he thought about what it would be like to be dead.

It was his special place that gave him courage and allowed him to think. The spot was out past the house, past the corn crib, across the back field and on the edge of the woods, deep in a tangled patch of sweetbriar so thick that it was impossible to see inside, much less get past its thorns. Half of it was growing out into the field, the rest of it fought with the woods for supremacy.

He would streak from the house and across the field, cut around the big thorny shrub to an overgrown path that led into the woods. Once in the trees, he would buttonhook back to the sweetbriar, entering from the woods side. It was fear that initially drove him under the briars and he paid the price for that. But he learned soon enough how to claw his thin frame carefully under the stickers to the center of the patch. There, with the help of his mother's old paring knife, he maintained open space that allowed him to look out over the field to the yard without being seen. Even if someone could ever see him, they wouldn't be fool enough to brave the thorns to try to get at him. More than once, he watched breathlessly as his father stormed after him, past his hiding place, and up the woodland track. He would wait silently until he heard Big Russ come back, swearing in drunken frustration, making the assumption that Ruddie had disappeared deep into the forest.

He gained some security from the hiding place and gleaned a little heart from it. When he first discovered his spiny sanctuary and he got the crying under control, he would lay back, stare up through the sweetbriar, and dream of having the courage to stand up to the likes of his father or the city boys in the alley who used to torment him.

Sometimes his dreams were of growing up and becoming like the men in the books his mother used to tell him about. Someone respected and feared. Someone like The Deerslayer—a man who was fierce and strong enough to make his own peace.

One time, Ruddie told his mother these things while making a face that he thought fierce and strong. She laughed and hugged him and told him that one day he would be big and strong. But then she held him at arm's length, looked into his eyes, patted his chest and told him that, first, he needed to be strong enough inside to keep going, to never give up.

Another time, when he asked her about his name, she told him that he was named after a famous writer who had written a poem about growing up strong. Again, she explained, it was not the strength of might but of heart.

Ruddie would think often about his mother. She was a dreamer, but not about being strong, at least not in the way Ruddie dreamed about being strong. Her dreams were more like those found in the books she brought with her from the city. The books that Big Russ burned one night in sodden anger when he came home and found her reading instead of making dinner. With his own dreams crushed, he sought to extinguish hers.

Ruddie knew all of the books—*Treasure Island, The Jungle Book, David Copperfield, The Adventures of Huckleberry Finn* and others. He knew them because, when they were gone, his mother would nurture him with the stories from memory. Whether it was Mowgli, Jim Hawkins, Davy or Huck, she passed on their lives, their lessons and the dreams of boys just like him. Dreams of strength of character.

Ruddie devoured it all without understanding a lot of it of course; but then he would anger his father for one reason or another. And, at those times, he knew the strength he wanted had more to do with muscle than moxie.

Inevitably, his dreams of strength would fade and the tears would come again. His sadness was born of the loss of his mother and sister and propelled by a primal fear of his father. He had loved his mother; she was everything to him. Anything he had or thought was good came from her. But, like her books, she was gone now.

Ruddie hated the farm and hated the work of a farmer. He feared being ground down by it, like gravel under the iron band on the wheels of their old corn wagon. The boy harbored other anxieties as well. He had little control over what happened to him and that made him edgy and watchful. Maybe the deepest dread of all, though, was the idea that nothing would ever change and he would live out his time and die on the Quick's godforsaken patch.

Ruddie didn't have the words to explain his thoughts, even if there was someone interested enough to ask. He was alone. And some of the time that was okay; but other times, when he felt alone, he would begin to think again about final rewards and the value of cashing-in early.

But all of those dark thoughts began to change one evening. Ruddie found himself once again dodging his father who had found the jug the boy had hidden from him in the corn crib. Tucked away in the thorns, Ruddie listened to a fading string of drunken curses, as Big Russ made his way down to the village road. Out of the corner of his eye, the boy caught a furtive movement off to his right. Through the sweetbriar, in the gathering dusk, he watched five furry balls emerge from a hole in the ground. Little brown things tumbling against each other, rolling over, nipping and making squeaking noises as they explored each other and the field immediately around the den. Fox kits!

Soon, a red fox emerged from the woods with something in her mouth. She was at least a couple of feet long with a beautiful brush tail that added another foot or so. Unlike her pups, she had a deep red coat, black paws and a distinctive white tip at the end of her tail. Her babies ignored whatever it was she dropped in front of them and fought each other to get at their mother's teats. At first, she let them have their way; and, as she did, she turned and stared into the sweetbriar thicket.

Ruddie sucked in his breath and stared back, head low, wondering whether he had been spotted. The fox turned to him full and let out a short bark, more of a huff really. Then, she ignored the concealed boy and began pushing her kits away from her, directing their attention to her prize, maybe a rodent of some sort. The little ones soon became absorbed with this new attraction, pouncing on the thing and setting up a chorus of noise in their efforts to subdue the inert body.

The boy watched the animals play for nearly an hour and, as the evening grew into night, he managed to see the fox gather her brood and herd them back down into the den. With his father gone, Ruddie emerged from the brush and, as he did, he noticed the vixen standing outside of the burrow watching him.

"That's a nice family you have there, Mrs. Fox," Ruddie said to her. Then he walked slowly across the field back to the house. Big Russ would not be home for a few hours.

That night, the boy lay on a thin mattress next to his mother's old cupboard, listening to the sounds of the farm and woods. Sleep was taking its time to come and he could not get the sight of the foxes out of his mind. They lived an ordered life and it seemed to him that the young ones worried little about the future. They were not dreamers, they lived in the moment and every moment was a new adventure. He saw a freedom in these things and he envied it.

The next day he woke with a start. He hadn't intended to be there when Big Russ got home, but now it was too late. He calmed himself by realizing his father probably just fell into bed dead to the world last night, rather than wake Ruddie up to punish him. So, the boy rose quietly and tip-toed across the room to the back door. But, as he did, he noticed the door to his parents' room standing open. A quick peek in told him that his father was not there. Since it was the man's habit to sleep later after he'd been drinking, Ruddie wondered whether he had come home at all last night. There was no sign of activity outside anywhere, so he went back inside, found a stale corn dodger and a piece of fat back and ate them hungrily.

Since it was his job to maintain the wood pile, the boy found the maul and wedge and trudged over to the logs that needed splitting. It was hard work for someone of his size, but it was far better to be found working than sitting around when his father got home.

An hour later, Ruddie first heard, then saw, a horse and buggy emerge from the woods road and onto the rutted track leading to the farm. He stood and watched, leaning on the maul. As he neared, the driver spotted him and waved. It wasn't a friendly wave, more like a "come here" wave.

Ruddie looked behind him to assure a means of escape, if necessary. He could run through the house, out the back, under the fence, around the crib and into the woods, turning into his thorny hideout. He looked to either side of him and waited, ready to move at the slightest whiff of danger.

The man ran the buggy right up to the boy, turning the sweating horse so that he could speak across the seat.

"This the Quick, place? They said it ain't much."

"I don't need you to tell me that, mister," answered Ruddie.

"You must be Russ Quick's boy, given your mouth and all that red hair."

"What do you want, mister?" Ruddie was on alert. He didn't like this fat man and the mention of his father could not be good.

"Boy, my name's Haupt, Sheriff Bill Haupt," he said, pulling his coat back to reveal a badge and his gun belt. "I'm looking for your daddy. Is he here?

"No, he ain't. Why do you want him?"

"Never mind, son, just get in," he answered. Then he kicked the long-step down for Ruddie. "I'll tell you on the way."

"On the way where? And, one more time, what do you want?"

With that, the sheriff made a grab at him, sprawling across the buggy's seat. But Ruddie was too fast. The man never got close. The youngster was under the fence and pelting across the field before the law had even gotten out of the buggy.

From the thicket, he watched Sheriff Haupt make a half-hearted effort to pursue him. The sheriff never saw the boy after the moment he ran into the house. So, he stopped at the back door and bawled:

"Boy! I ain't gonna hurt ya. It's about your daddy. Boy!"

The sheriff quickly assumed that Ruddie had disappeared into the woods and was long gone. So, he shook his head, shrugged and left.

Ruddie stayed hidden for the rest of the day, all that night, and into the next morning. He slept some and amused himself watching the red fox and her charges. He noticed her begin to teach them foraging skills, hiding food in catches and making them use their eyes and noses to find it. She would disappear to hunt, but return soon after with an array of prey. He saw a squirrel, a mole or something like it, a couple of birds, and even a frog. At one point, he saw her emerge from the corn crib with a rat.

He was fascinated by her tactics. Each time she returned, the treasure was buried in locations farther and farther from the den. The kits in their search often found themselves spread out and alone in the field or woods. While the fox would eventually call to those who were lost, she was more focused on introducing them to the independent life they would have to lead by the end of the summer and the onset of fall.

About midmorning, Ruddie's hunger drove him back to the house. There, he used the well to deal with his thirst, then ate the last of the fat back and finished off the last two rock-like dodgers. He was pulling his filthy shirt over his head when he heard the snap of a stick. When he pulled it back down, he could see a man coming toward the front door and another approaching the side window. There would soon be a third at the back door.

Ruddie arrived there at the same time Sheriff Haupt did. But Haupt was too slow to react to the boy darting under his arm and squeezing through the narrow passage the sheriff was trying to block with his bulk. The man turned in time to see his prey high-tailing it to the back woods. And while he didn't bother to run himself, he directed his deputies. "Catch the little bastard!"

They were young men and they were on his heels, but the fence slowed them.

Ruddie reached the woods; then, in the trees' shadow, he turned and slid into his refuge. Lying flat, listening, he peered out and saw the men halt their pursuit at the start of the wood's path.

"Christ! I'm not running after that kid into these trees; he could be anywhere. To hell with that porky sumbitch. Let him chase him."

"Roy, I thought you were the one bucking for a promotion."

"It makes no sense. Tomorrow, we can come back with the dogs. It's a waste of my time."

"What else you got to do?"

"Nothin', but the sheriff says maybe the boy knows where Quick went or, if we hold the kid, maybe Big Russ will come back for him, like bait. Truth is, he ain't never comin' back here, if he's smart. That miner's dead and there's witnesses saw Quick stab him."

"Yeah and those witnesses, say Big Russ picked the fight, then went at ole Jim from behind. Never saw it coming. Quick should hang for it, I'd say."

"Oh, so you're a judge now, huh? I thought you were an adjunct assistant deputy sheriff."

"I'm just sayin' ..."

"Let's go. We'll give the hounds a run at the boy tomorrow."

The men turned and made their way back to the house. The sheriff waited for them, then began shouting and waving his arms until one of the men started talking. After listening with hands on hips, he pointed at his deputy, spoke to him with an edge, then signaled for them to leave.

Again, Ruddie stayed in the thorns all that day, but he didn't sleep and he wasn't interested in the foxes. *His father was gone? Wanted for murder? What did it mean?* He felt a burden lift, then was crushed with fear. They were coming back the next day with their blue hounds.

He was all alone and felt like crying, but he didn't. He had to make a decision and bawling wouldn't help. He had to leave for good because the dogs would find him, even in the thorns. But where would he go, how would he make his way?

Without answers, the boy sat frozen in his situation, knowing he was running out of time. He stared out of the thicket into nothing, but before long, he began to notice the foxes. He saw that there were only four of the pups and the vixen was urging them away from the den, refusing to allow them to enter and sending them off with a nip or a cuff.

After a while, two kits returned to the burrow to find their mother as uncooperative as she was the first time, maybe a little less so. He watched this drama over the afternoon until dusk when the red fox waited to see if her pups would return. Finally, she rose and began kicking dirt and debris into the burrow. Then, with a flick of her tail, she trotted off in a direction opposite those taken by her progeny.

As the evening lengthened, Ruddie knew what he would do. He would leave it all behind and travel, foraging as he went. If he needed to, he would find work. Where he was going became less important than the fact that he was going. The unknown was less frightening than what he knew would happen if he stayed. The fox kits and their mother had schooled him.

CHAPTER 2

FREEDOM

Ruddie had been walking for two long days, staying off the roads, using seldom traveled farm tracks, and skirting any sign of people. He went under fences rather than over them, avoided rises that would offer a silhouette against the sky, and stayed within the cover of woods whenever he could. His bare feet were hardened but they hurt and he was as hungry as he had ever remembered being. Once, he came across wild blueberries, another time he pilfered a few handfuls of cherries from a lonely orchard. Ears of new corn were also his for the taking. But the pickings were not yet ripe and at first it was just a bellyache, then later he found himself squatting in pain.

The late afternoon sky was leaden and had the feel of rain when the boy stopped just inside the woods bordering a clearing. Staying in the shadows, he stood stock still, peering out over a small field to a clapboard farmhouse and a stained barn marked with a faded red hex sign. A couple of outbuildings also in need of paint flanked the barn. One of them was a chicken coop.

Ruddie was hungry enough to take a risk and an armful of hen's eggs sounded worth it. But he wasn't so desperate that he would dare a raid in daylight. The fugitive would watch and wait until dark, get an idea of the farm, the house, and the people who lived there. Who knows, maybe he wouldn't even have to steal the eggs.

He tucked in under a pile of deadfall at the wood's edge. It would afford at least some cover from the coming rain that he now could smell on a building breeze. From his burrow he had a clear view of the farmyard across the field.

Within a few minutes, a woman emerged from the house with a basket. Two grimy little girls, each with a shock of wild blond hair, pushed past her and fell upon a bare patch of dirt where they began to fight over a hopscotch heel. The woman began dragging laundry from a sagging line as fat drops of rain started to fall. As she dropped the laundry into her basket, she bawled something at the squabbling girls. The kids played on, ignoring her.

Ruddie sat back and pushed his meager bindle behind him for comfort, careful not to lay on his mother's knife hidden there. He hunched his shoulders, trying to stay as dry as he could under the brush, and waited.

When the clothesline was bare, the woman attempted to shoo the girls back inside, out of the increasing rain. But the girls were now fully engaged in their game, oblivious to the wet and their mother. The woman drew herself up to deliver a more forceful order when her attention was drawn toward a nearby cornfield. There, a raw-boned man whose bare chest was covered only by the bib of his overalls, was emerging out of the rows of stalks. He carried a pair of long-handled hay rakes over his shoulder. Two gangly boys followed him, one was a teenager, the other younger.

Ruddie watched the bigger boy trip his companion and push him down hard. The bully laughed as the boy tumbled over, breaking several corn stalks in the process. The farmer reacted quickly by cuffing the back of the older boy's head.

"Curtis, we ain't so rich that we can waste good corn like that. Now, help your brother up," the man commanded.

The teen didn't move. Instead, he gave his father a black, resentful look, then ducked when the man took a fuller swing at him.

"That's okay, Poppa," said the smaller boy. "I'm alright."

"He don't give a damn about you, Albie," said the older boy. "It's the corn he cares about."

"Curtis ..." started the father.

But the teen already had begun to run and when he passed one of the girls, he yanked her hair, making her howl. With that last bit of meanness, he bolted up the steps and disappeared into the house. The rest of the family soon followed in a trot to avoid the intensifying shower.

The rain was a short squall, but it was enough to create a steady drip within Ruddie's hideout, some of it finding its way down the back of his neck. Just the same, he sat quietly, unseen. When the rain stopped, he watched the family perform those chores that readied the place for the night. He observed the farmer secure the barn and the henhouse, noting the coop's noisy gate. His stomach groaned as he heard a call to dinner through an open window, then endured the faint sounds of rattling plates, knives, spoons and the meal being eaten. But he had to be patient because he needed darkness and he needed the farmer to fall asleep first. With guile and luck, he would be eating an egg or two tonight.

The moon lit the woods in dull silver and gave the awn of the still-green corn an eerie glow. Ruddie watched the silk shimmer as the night breathed in and out. The moonlight was a problem, but the thief was not going to let it stop him. He was undiscovered in his crouching lope across the yard to the henhouse gate. He struggled briefly with the wire loop that held the thing closed but managed to minimize noise by only opening the barrier a few inches, then sliding through.

Once inside, Ruddie stayed calm and gently poked around for eggs, relieved that the five birds nesting there were being relatively quiet. But there were no eggs to be found and probably wouldn't be until morning. He realized that he would have to take one of the hens if he was going to eat.

Stealing a chicken was something he was trying to avoid. He hated dealing with the birds. It would be a lot of trouble—killing it, gutting it, plucking it, and building a fire to roast it. All former tasks of his on the farm. And it meant he would have to get far away before he could eat. A farmer with only five chickens would surely miss one and was likely to come looking for whatever critter took it. In the end, the taste might make it all worthwhile, but it was a pain and it would slow him down. Besides, it was really stealing, not just nipping a few eggs.

But Ruddie was hungry, so he worked through these considerations in a flash and grabbed the nearest bird by the neck. This set the other hens to squawking, but he was out the door in a jump. As he eased through the enclosure's gate, he sensed rather than saw a dark shadow loom up from around the side of the coop. When he turned, the shadow spoke.

"Where you going with my chicken, boy?"

A red pinpoint glowed from the head of the silhouette and the smell of burning corn silk wafted over Ruddie.

"Good thing, I like to take my leisure out here, huh, boy? A good way to catch thieving varmints trying to take from us," said the teenager Ruddie saw earlier.

With that, his arm snaked out and grabbed the chicken. His other hand buried itself in the poacher's shirt and threw him to the ground. Sitting on top of the boy and putting a knee in his back, Curtis grabbed a fist full of red hair and pushed Ruddie's head down into dirt that smelled of chicken droppings.

"Before I turn you over to my Poppa, I'm going to have a little fun with you. If you had been a fox or a possum, I'd have just killed you; but now I get to enjoy myself."

The teen held the ersatz cigarette in his mouth, squinting to avoid the smoke drifting from the butt. With his free hand he gave a good pull on the corn silk, then touched it to the back of his victim's neck. Ruddie yelped, and squirmed but was held firm. When the teen burned him a second time, the boy rolled right, then left, then right again, shifting his tormentor's weight and throwing him off. Ruddie leapt up but was grabbed by the ankle and tripped back down. Because Curtis still held the bird, he couldn't control his captive. So, Ruddie flipped over and delivered a vicious kick to the bridge of the farm boy's nose.

Curtis dropped both the chicken and Ruddie's foot, both hands flying to his broken nose. The released hen bolted away, setting up a loud racket and inducing the rest of its flock to do the same. Ruddie scrambled up and broke for the woods. When he did, he saw the farmer emerge from the house and yell "Hey!" A moment later a shotgun boomed.

Ruddie ducked reflexively, rather late after hearing the pellets rip over his head. He ran faster than he ever had in his life and reached the trees as the man fired the second barrel into the brush a few feet to the left of him. In full panic, the boy plunged into the trees but, not ten feet in, he tripped over a fallen branch and tumbled into a patch of arrowwood. There he lay praying that the farmer would not pursue him into the woods. He looked back to see the man swat Curtis as the teen came up onto the porch, crying about his nose. The farmer then looked at his son, put his arm around him, and led him back into the house.

Ruddie shook with the residual shock that comes from being shot at. He knelt up and hugged himself, taking stock. He was now exhausted, terrified and hungrier than he was an hour ago. His neck stung as well.

As his breathing and his heart began to slow, the boy recalled seeing something odd as he fled. Maybe he had imagined it, but between the first and second shotgun blast, he noticed a long, low shadow steal from the other side of the hen house. At first it ran with him to the woods; then, just inside, it stopped and dropped something. Hesitating for a split second, the shadow then disappeared into one of the rows of nearby corn.

Ruddie crept back to the edge of the woods, keeping his eye on the house. There, in the moon's weak light, he noticed a small dark pile. He reached for it and his hand found feathers and the still-warm body of the pilfered chicken. Its neck had been neatly snapped. He knew then that it was, in fact, a fox that had left him a present.

A week or so later, Ruddie found himself at the base of a forested mountain. He didn't know which had been harder—the climb up or the tricky descent down through the deadfall and boulders. He managed to survive with only skinned knees and a few bruises but determined to stick to valleys in the future. After his long nights on the tramp, Ruddie decided that freedom in the wild could be very lonely and very scary. The night was full of noises, animals hunting or animals being hunted. It made sleep uncertain. Maybe he was far enough away now, and maybe a few other people wouldn't be so bad. The valleys were where they would be, not on top of some mountain.

He emerged in daylight from the trees covering the height behind him. The boy's furtive reconnaissance had produced no sign of danger. So, he crossed a dirt footpath and walked out into a grassy meadow. The pasture covered a point of land that ran a ways, then seemed to end abruptly in thin air. He was out in the open and soon enough realized that he had put himself in a box with only one way out. Then his ears pricked up at a strange sound. It was almost a low hum or drone of some kind, an indistinct mash, made up of multiple sounds.

The spooked boy immediately dropped down on his stomach and pulled his bindle in close. He froze, listening intently. He could now distinguish the clanging of iron, the braying of mules, the shouts of men and a number of other sounds he couldn't identify. Lying face down, Ruddie could smell the wild onion growing in the thick grass. He also picked up a whiff of burning coal and maybe wood smoke as well. Finally, his nose found that unique, burnt, iron-like smell produced by sparks or electricity. He felt the sun on his neck, the grasshopper that landed on his foot, and the slight breeze that carried the sounds and the smells.

After a few moments of lying stock-still, Ruddie's curiosity propelled him closer to the edge of the field. Maintaining caution, he began to crawl toward the noise. Suddenly, the air around him was split wide open with a deafening scream, then another. He covered his ears with his hands and dropped flat into the thick grass once more.

Ruddie was about to bolt back to cover in the woods when someone spoke to him. "What's a matter, boy? Never heard a train whistle before? Nothin' to be afraid of. No, nothing at all."

Ruddie's head shot up and not ten feet away, unseen before, was an ancient black man sitting on a rickety bench. He was as skinny as they come, hoary with age and sporting a shock of white hair that covered his head like a nimbus. His face was weathered and cracked, with little black dots peppering his high cheek bones. He appeared to be missing a great many teeth because his face looked to be collapsing in on itself, like an apple left too long on the windowsill.

The bench that held him was made of rough tree limbs, nailed together in an indifferent way. The dilapidated seat had been placed to afford a view of whatever was on the other side of the bluff.

"Here. Come look. That was the B&O's No. 205 engine. Just telling the folks in the Cumberland Station that they've arrived on time."

The old man smiled, moved over on the bench, and waved Ruddie over.

The boy stood cautiously, looking all around him. He could see that they were alone and Ruddie couldn't imagine the old man was quick enough or strong enough to be a threat. He edged over with one eye on his host and one on whatever he was about to see over the edge of the scarp. He moved behind the bench, keeping it between him and the geezer. When he looked up and out over the bluff, he took an inadvertent step back and gawked, issuing an animal sound of fear and surprise.

"Amazing, isn't it, boy?"

Ruddie couldn't speak. What he saw was a heart-stopping, chaotic scene that reminded him of the end of the world, like the picture in his mother's Bible. There was hellish, frenetic movement everywhere he looked. To his right, a sooty city rose from a river valley ringed by ancient, round-shouldered mountains. Gritty, brick warehouses wore an apron of industry that ran down to teeming river boat piers, canal docks, and rail yards. Behind all of this commerce, a number of pious church spires sprouted and above it all, a gleaming domed structure could be seen, as the city climbed the surrounding foothills.

"That's Cumberland, the Queen City, you're looking at. She's been here from the days when the only ones here were Indians. Used to be a fort too. Washington himself was here as a colonel when we were fightin' the French. Wagons, boats, and trains have been pushing through this gap in the Appalachians, west into Ohio and beyond, ever since."

Ruddie was only half-listening to the history lesson because his eyes had swiveled to the panorama directly over the edge of the field. He saw a huge locomotive train belching black smoke, dragging a long line of cars up a track that ran into the city. Behind the rail right-of-way, he saw a wide berm rise to a dirt road and a huge waterway flowing beside it. Both the road and the water were jammed with boats, goods of all sorts, mules, and gesturing men. The canal must have had at least thirty long freight boats, strung out in queues in both directions. Some were headed for the city and waiting their turn to get through a gate-like structure that bore a big number seventy-five painted on it. Others were going in the opposite direction, pulled by mules and laden with what looked like coal. Some boats were docked, unloading cargo, feeding their mules, or putting in for the night. But to Ruddie, it was pandemonium, overwhelming and frightening. He was a young boy who had really only known the farm. In front of him was the world.

"Please, young man, come sit down. Take a load off. By the looks of them, those feet of yours could use a rest. Come to think of it, you seem a little worse for wear in general. When was the last time you had something to eat? Got any food in that bindle of yours? Here, take a drink of my water."

The elder lifted what looked like an old Union Army canteen with a wooden stopper from the bench and extended it to the boy.

Ruddie, without looking away from the frenzied scene laid out before him, moved around the bench, sat, and thankfully accepted the water.

"It's been a day or so, sir. A woman I met up on the mountain was kind to me and gave me a johnnycake and fatback." A thumb over his shoulder indicated the mountain behind them that he had just crawled down.

"You were up on ole Knobly Mountain, boy? That must have been Kate Two Owls you met, one of the last Shawnees livin' around here. Maybe one of the last Shawnees, period. Kate's an old friend of mine and as kind as they come."

"What is all of that out there, mister?" asked Ruddie, now standing on his toes and looking out over his nose. "I can't make heads or tails of it. Never seen the like."

The black man laughed heartily at that, but his mirth was interrupted by a wracking cough that took him a minute to get under control. Once he was able to settle back on his bench, he rasped, "Like I said, no need to be afraid. That's America flexing her muscles. Working men and women, just finding ways to get along. Like you and me."

The old man reached into a pocket of a patched coat, threadbare at the sleeves and elbows. With the flourish of a deft magician, he produced a yellow corn dodger and a hunk of white cheese. He broke both in two and with a smile offered half to Ruddie.

"Mister, that's awful generous of you, but I can't take that. Ma said never to take from those who don't have. You look like you don't have too much."

The old man laughed again. "Boy, I already have all I need. You go on and take this. While you're chewing on it, I'll explain what you're looking at and then you won't be so scared."

Ruddie was taken in by the man's gentle way, so he sat and hungrily ate the gifts he was given and listened to the voice of experience.

"I guess it can be confusing if you don't know what you're looking at, but I spent a lot of years down there working as a fireman on the B&O's trains. Spent a fair amount of time on canal boats as well. Even rode the Potomac down to Washington, DC a few times. The Potomac River is that wide strip of silver you can see way in the distance, beyond the canal. That there canal is the Chesapeake and Ohio; runs alongside of the river all the way up here from Little Falls, outside our nation's capital. They finished all 185 miles of the Grand Old Ditch back in 1850, before the war. When I was on the water, we carried everything from Allegheny coal down the canal to salted fish and Chesapeake oysters up the canal. These days, it's all coal because the B&O owns it all and coal is what makes the most money."

Once again, the old man was tormented by a nasty cough that forced a pause in his soliloquy. Ruddie looked at his companion and wondered if he should do something. Eventually the elder got things under control once more, but seemed drained by the effort, offering a weak, apologetic smile.

"Mister, are you alright?" asked the boy. "Can I get you something?"

"No, son, I've got the black lung and there's nothing to be done. I come up here to remember the old days and to await my maker."

Ruddie was not sure what any of that meant, but it couldn't be good. So, he said nothing and sat looking at the activity below him. The two remained in silence for a few minutes while the old man recovered and the young boy began to sort out the scene that now was more fascinating than scary. He managed to distinguish the three great industrial arenas that paralleled each other – the river, the canal, and the railroad.

After a time, the old man asked, "Son, where are you headed all by yourself?"

"Well, sir, I'm not exactly sure. I guess I'm looking for a way to get along, like you say."

"No folks to go home to?"

"Nope," was the only answer Ruddie offered.

"Well, if you are going to feed yourself, that usually means finding work. Otherwise, you'll be doing a lot of running from those who don't like the idea of you borrowing meals."

The boy didn't look up at the man, but he knew exactly what he was saying. The memory of that farmer's shotgun was still fresh.

"I could find work. I'm stronger than I look and I know what it is to work hard."

"I believe you, boy. If I had a job to give you, I would. As it is, any jobs to be had are down there," said the old man, pointing over the bluff.

Ruddie had been bowled over by the power and majesty of the locomotive that had rolled by and he was immediately smitten by the mechanical monster. "I wouldn't mind working on the railroad," he commented, not revealing how excited he really was by the idea.

"A job like that is out of reach for you, son. Maybe one day you will be a railroader, but not today. That work requires grown men and then there's the union. No, you better think about something else for now."

Ruddie was disappointed, but that feeling was not new to him. There wasn't very much in his short life that was within his grasp. So, he did what he usually did by deciding that railroading probably wasn't all that great a job anyway. Noisy, dirty, and hard.

"What about working on a canal boat? I can shovel coal. I even know mules. My daddy used to have the loan of a mule come spring planting."

"Well, that's a possibility. But you'd have to find yourself an older, private-owned boat. Most of them now belong to the B&O and they're not going to hire a sprite like you."

"Where would I find one of these private boats?"

The older man rose slowly from the bench, leaning on a stout cane, carved with an ornate parrot's head and tipped with silver. Ruddie was surprised to see the old man with such a fine walking stick.

"If I were you, I'd look for a boat that had a name. A real name, not one of the numbered boats owned by the railroad. Usually, if you find a barge like that, you'll find a family operating it. They might hire you on. That's what my grandson did."

"He has a job on a canal boat?"

"He sure does, but it's not all just walking the towpath. It's hard work and the days are long. I'm a little worried about him. His folks are gone now and he's not that big a boy. That's really what I'm doing up here today."

"Sir …?"

"In a few minutes, a canal boat named the *Minnie B. Welcome* will be putting in right there at that landing below us. My kin should be on it and I want to see if I can find out how he's doing. I've got to get going."

With that, the old man laid a huge, gnarled hand on the boy's shoulder and said, "I'd like to leave you with something to think about. Don't give up on your dreams. If you want to be a railroad man, then work toward that, in time you may get what you want. I did."

Ruddie watched the ancient man walk stiffly to the dirt path and, with the help of the fancy cane, disappear around a bend. The boy was puzzled by the old man's words. Dreams? He had no dreams other than those of a boy. What little experience he had with dreams taught him that they can be painful things.

Chapter 3

The Arrival of the *Minnie B. Welcome*

Ruddie laid in the grass at the edge of the bluff. He saw that he was not atop a sheer cliff, but above an easily navigated slope that ran down to a fence, topped with barbed wire. The barrier enclosed the railroad right-of-way that held tracks, a few storage sheds, and spare materials piled along the rails. The area was strewn with general trash and other refuse of the rail industry.

Far off, he could see the sun on boats plying the wide river. Nearer, the canal's daily work of docking, loading, and unloading went on. The freight boats and piers swarmed with working men and women. Drays, wagons, and carts clogged the road from the docks to the city. The tow path tracing the canal was crowded with teams of mules dragging their waterborne burdens.

Ruddie watched people spill in and out of businesses that lined the waterway and the railroad yards. He wondered again why his family chose to live on a farm and why his father couldn't find a job here among all of this bustle. The boy was happier to see other people than he thought he would be. It had been almost two weeks of solitude and living like a furtive animal. He had survived on a skinny chicken, a hunk of cheese, near-ripe cherries, the occasional apple and the green corn that was everywhere. His belly paid the price for his diet of course, but it had kept him from starving.

Thinking once again about food, he recalled the one night he managed to find a decent meal. It had been two burnt potatoes and a slab of gristly steak, found in the garbage behind a ramshackle hotel. By the time this meal was gone, he was convinced that living wild didn't offer the freedom he thought it did. Freedom is alright, he guessed, when there was food to eat. Freedom was too lonely as well. He knew now that he would try to find work—somewhere that offered things to do, real meals and people who were not looking for him. The canal was the place.

As the boy worked this out, he noticed that there was no fence separating the railroad from the canal, so it was just one fence he had to scale in order to get over the tracks and up the berm to the boats. He was looking for a way over the barrier when he saw two men walking purposefully along the railroad tracks. They wore red union suits under filthy blue overalls and dusty derby hats. They carried what looked like clubs which periodically they would twirl offhandedly. Their harsh laughter showed white teeth under heavy black mustaches. Ruddie didn't know it at the time, but they were yard bulls at their work.

The coarse humor stopped abruptly once they reached a cluster of worn storage sheds along the rail. There, they threw open doors and could be heard banging things around inside. When they came to a third shed, the larger of the two men stayed outside while his partner entered the space. Immediately, a yell of warning was heard and a raggedy, bearded man bolted from the little building.

The bull waiting outside was ready. As the vagrant flashed by him, he swung the club, catching the fleeing man under the chin, clotheslining him and flipping him over on to his back. The interloper twisted and shakily rose to all fours, then received a boot in the ribs, rolling him back over in the dirt. When the second rail guard emerged, he added a hard jab in the stomach with his own billy and a few more kicks to drive home the "no trespassing" message. The beaten man lay motionless and the bulls backed off. The hobo had some sand though because as soon as the toughs stepped back, he sprang up and made a beeline toward the barbed wire fence. Ruddie watched as the goons gave chase, but the fugitive knew where a hole had been cut in the fence and he disappeared through it rapidly and into the brush on the other side.

The railroad men ran to the hole, decided that it wasn't worth the effort to chase the bum, tried in vain to pull the cut wire together, then agreed it was best left to the maintenance crew. With a shrug, they began an uninterested stroll back down the tracks and away.

Ruddie guessed that if he was going to brave crossing the railroad property here, now was the time to do it. He made his way down from the meadow to the hole in the fence. Once through, he stayed close to the wall of one of the rotting sheds, keeping it between himself and the departing guards. He edged to the building's corner, then darted, low, across open ground, strewn with the kind of debris that accumulates along railroad tracks. A jumble of ties, black with creosote, afforded him some cover. What he didn't notice were several empty tin cans that had accumulated below the pile. As he slid behind the mound, he managed to kick a few of the noisy things and one even rolled out from behind his hiding place. His heart stopped when he saw the men turn and look backward.

Ruddie crouched frozen for what felt like an hour while the men continued to stare. When one of them made the decision to investigate, the wide-eyed boy was about to make a run for it back through the hole in the fence. That's when the bull's partner said something about rats, then something else about lunch. This ended any interest in exploring the stinking pile of wood.

Once the men were gone, Ruddie hopped over the train tracks, slid down a gravel embankment and scrambled up to the top of the wide berm. This earthen work was the support for the concrete and stone construction that was the C&O Canal. He found thick laurel growing above the busy waterway and used it to get his bearings without being seen. He had gotten past the railroad guards, but Ruddie stayed cautious and hidden.

The *Minnie B. Welcome* was now putting in at the landing below him, just as the old man had said it would. The ninety-foot boat was coming in slowly, timing the departure of a like vessel being towed away from the same landing. A bandy-legged man in suspenders with his sleeves rolled barked directions to a woman working the tiller. A filthy little girl in a sack dress played happily with a doll, oblivious to the rope that tied her to a cleat on the roof of the long boat's cabin.

The boatman then began to curse harshly, berating a young man in a slouch hat and a barefoot, black boy. They were on the towpath, struggling with two very upset mules. The young man was furious with the animals and began to beat their rumps with a switch. As the mules twisted in harness to avoid the abuse, they shifted and side-stepped, putting the boy behind them. That's when one of the distressed beasts launched a kick that sent the kid slamming into the landing's feedbox ten feet away.

The ruckus was heard by the animals towing the vacating boat and, mules being creatures that refuse to put themselves in any kind of danger, stopped. This killed any departing momentum the boat was building. At the same time, the excited *Minnie B. Welcome* mules attempted to bolt while still attached to the towline, increasing the craft's arrival speed.

Ruddie watched in fascination as one boat's prow nudged in close between the landing and the departing stern. There was no crash, but it was close. So close that the *Minnie B. Welcome*'s slack towline caught a rear stanchion on the exiting boat as its mules decided to pull again.

The *Minnie B. Welcome*'s pilot spotted the tangle and began to howl, waving his arms and running the raceway along the rail to the fore of the boat. Ruddie didn't know what to make of that until he watched with horror as the departing barge dragged the *Minnie B. Welcome* mules slowly but surely into the canal, between the boats. Halfway down the plank, the pilot stopped, balled his hands in his hair and sank to his knees in anguish. The young man on the towpath panicked, grabbed the halter of one of the terrified animals and began yanking it. His efforts had no effect on the sliding mules and only succeeded in tangling his arm in the halter. That's when the woman at the tiller screamed.

Ruddie sat petrified, aghast as he watched the young man and the two mules disappear over the stone wall of the landing and into the water. The young man, mules, harness and towlines churned in a boiling, repulsive cauldron of noise and terror. The woman wailed, the little girl began to cry, and men all around the landing ran to the accident.

Ruddie was stunned as he watched bodies and ropes intertwine and the terrified animals kick and flail in the roiling water. As bad a scene as that was, Ruddie was most shocked by the first kick the mule had delivered to the little boy. He realized that the kid could be the old man's grandson. He remembered the elder's kindness and knew he had to get down there. He leapt up and tore down the hill to the towpath.

CHAPTER 4

BIRD

The towpath and the landing wall were crowded with frantic people watching the horrific, convulsing turbulence between the boats. The water looked to be only four or five feet deep, but the tangled mules' terror-stricken efforts to stand upright and keep their heads above water only wove the mass of mule and man together tighter. The young man's limp and bloody body was tumbled over and over by the wildly thrashing beasts.

Ruddie ran past a bearded man who swung an axe down on the strangling towrope of the *Minnie B. Welcome.* Two other men attempted to snag the lines and the bodies caught in the maelstrom between boats. A short man was joined by a powerful looking woman, as they threw their weight behind a pole, trying to keep the two boats apart.

Ruddie spotted the boy lying in a heap below the landing's mule feeder box. He started to him, but was blocked by an angry, arriving contingent from the boat that had gotten caught up in the slack towline. They were pointing and berating the *Minnie B.'s* pilot in broken, accented English, but left off as they became aware of the situation. Then, they started to argue among themselves over whose fault the accident was even as the horror in the water continued.

"You, okay? You, okay?", Ruddie asked the little boy, reaching him and shaking him by the shirt sleeve.

"Oww!" the boy yelled. "Leave me be!"

"I saw that mule kick you! That was really something! You coulda been killed! You sure you're okay?" Ruddie didn't know what to do but he wanted to do something. "Can I get someone to help?"

"Not unless they know how to fix a broken arm."

"You sure it's broken? Let me see." Ruddie thought he knew something about broken arms. He had helped his mother with hers that time.

"I said get off! Leave me alone. You ain't no doctor!" Then, he seemed to realize something. "George! I've got to see what happened to George!" The boy attempted to stand but the pain drove him back to sitting. He hugged his left arm and rocked back and forth.

Ruddie heard someone yelling that a doctor was on his way. So, he said, "Look, they've called a doctor for your friend. I'll get him to look at your arm too."

The farm boy pulled from his cloth sack a wide swath of burlap he had been using to cover the ground at night. Tearing it, he made a sling like the one his mother had shown him how to make. Ignoring the protests, he cradled the young boy's arm in its folds and tied a knot behind his head to secure it.

"That should help for a few minutes. Take the weight off, keep it still. The doctor's likely to be busy when he gets here. We may have to wait a bit. It must really hurt. Go ahead and cry if you want." Ruddie was excited and talking a blue streak.

Ruddie's patient stared daggers at him. There was no trace of a tear.

"What you doin' here, cracker?" asked the insulted boy.

"I ... I don't know. I'm just trying to help."

The two boys sat, backs against the feed box on the towpath, watching the chaos in front of them. Neither spoke. A man pushed his way through people to the landing wall and identified himself as an officer of the B&O Railroad and Canal. He raised a big Springfield bolt action rifle and shot one of the mules in the head, killing it. The boom of the gun made the boys jump. Then there was the sound of the bolt action slamming home again and another loud roar from the rifle rattled the boys a second time. After that, the water stopped churning and the men with the hooks began dragging the mess toward the wall. The bark of the rifle had startled the arguing men as well. They stopped pushing and shoving each other to gawk at the scene.

The futile attempt at rescue managed to separate George from the mule's harness. When hands pulled him up out of the water and over the wall of the canal, it was clear the young mule driver was dead. A man with a black bag pushed through the crowd and knelt over the victim briefly. Then he stood and pronounced the expected verdict. The woman who had stood at the *Minnie B. Welcome*'s tiller climbed down, let out one more wail of anguish and fell in great sobs on the battered body. The pilot of the unlucky craft remained on his knees, atop the boat, midway down the hatches. He was weeping in helpless silence.

After a bit, Ruddie got up as he saw the man with the black bag walk free of the people on the landing. Pointing to the boy, he caught the doctor's attention and brought him over. After a cursory examination, the man diagnosed a broken arm, said that it had to be set and gave the boy a business card.

"Come see me today at this address," he said, striding away to the carriage in which he had arrived.

Ruddie helped the boy to his feet and together they walked toward the *Minnie B. Welcome*.

"What's your name?" Ruddie eventually asked his temporary charge.

After some hesitation the young boy said, "Name's Horatio Dewitt Clinton Garrett, but they call me 'Bird.'"

"That's one heck of a name. Horatio what?"

"Dewitt Clinton Garrett. My grandpa gave me that name. Said it was after the man who built the Erie Canal. He also said the Garretts built the B&O Railroad."

"That's an awfully big name for somebody your size."

"I'm big enough, farm boy, or whatever you are. You don't look so high and mighty yourself."

"I wasn't sayin'—"

"Yes, you were, everybody does, that's why they call me Bird, sometimes Little Black Bird. I ain't dumb, I know what they're sayin'."

"Look, anyway, my name is Rudyard Quick, Ruddie for short."

"And you're laughing at my name?"

The boys had reached the side of the *Minnie B. Welcome* where the canal boat's master, his wife, and their little girl were clutching each other over the covered body of George.

"George was their boy, their only son. They loved him but they didn't really know the bastard."

Ruddie looked at Bird and knew he had been living hard under George's thumb. He even saw some degree of satisfaction or maybe relief in the boy's face.

Kindly people began to secure the *Minnie B. Welcome* and an official looking man drew the grieving family away to a quieter place along the towpath. Bird and Ruddie followed them to a pine table and benches under a white oak. The boys stood with others behind the tree and listened.

"Oh, Lucas what are we going to do now? Our George is gone," sobbed the woman.

Before the pilot could respond, the official said, "Mr. Twigg, sorry about your boy. Your boat's secure and my men will pull the mules out of there for you. No charge, but we keep the meat. You okay with that?"

When Twigg nodded with resignation, the local man continued. "You can have the berth until tomorrow night. I'm awfully sorry, but after that, you have to be moving along. Them's the rules as you know. Oh, yeah. One more thing. The sheriff said he wanted to talk to you."

Nodding once more to the dock man, Twigg comforted his wife. "Molly, I don't know what we're going to do. I do know that we have to swallow this, as hard as it may be. I think maybe a prayer that George is in a happier place right now is what we should do at the moment. You know he hated the canal."

Then Lucas Twigg held Molly's hands and they put their heads together in misery. Everyone listening bowed in prayer as well.

But no prayer was said before Molly tore away. "I just can't pray right now, Lucas. I am so angry. God has forgotten us. First, trouble with the boat's loan, then the loss of the grain contract down to Georgetown, we lose our son and our last two mules, and now the sheriff wants to talk to you. What have we done to be punished so?"

"Molly, I don't know. But we have to push on somehow. We still have our Ruthie." He drew the little girl in under his arm.

After a moment, Twigg said, "With George gone, I'm going to have to hire some help. We can't do it all ourselves. And I need to find two new mules before tomorrow night as well. I guess I'll add the animals to the supplies we were going to buy."

"We can't afford no hired hand, much less two mules," his wife fretted.

"You heard the man; we have to be gone by tomorrow night. If I have to borrow against the boat's cargo to buy or rent mules, I guess that's what I'll have to do. The sheriff can find me if he wants me."

Twigg looked up from his sorrow to begin his fight back to normal life when he noticed Bird and Ruddie standing behind the oak.

"Where have you been, boy? Those mules were your responsibility! Where the hell were you? My George is dead!" said the man in rising fury. He stood, reached for the frightened boy and raised a hand.

"Mr. Twigg, sir, I was hurt—" started the boy, ducking.

"Wait!" shouted Molly Twigg. "Don't hit him. He looks hurt."

At the same time, Ruddie stepped in front of Bird and threw up both hands. "He's telling the truth. I saw one of your mules kick him across the path."

"And just who the hell are you?" demanded Twigg.

"I'm nobody, sir, but your hired hand here has a broken arm according to the doctor that looked at it. Told Bird to see him in his office."

"That's just great," groused the boatman. "Now I have to pay for a broken arm. I don't have time for this. I've got to see about mules. Bird, you've been a good worker, but now ..." he hesitated. "But now I've got to let you go."

This hit Bird like a fist. But Mrs. Twigg said, "Lucas! You can't do that. The boy's hurt and he needs a doctor. We'll get it covered somehow." Then she asked Bird if he was in a lot of pain and drew him over to her. The boy came readily.

"Well, I don't have time to see no doctor with a little pickaninny like Bird. And as long as he can't do his work, he won't get paid." With that, Mr. Twigg turned and hunched away in the direction of the buildings along the canal.

"I'll go with Bird to the doctor's," offered Ruddie.

"Who are you again?" asked the woman.

"I hadn't said, ma'am, my name is Ruddie, Ruddie Quick. I know Bird's family."

The boy looked up in surprise at Ruddie's lie but before he could say anything, the redhaired stranger took him in hand and was propelling him after Mr. Twigg. "We'll be back as soon as we can," called Ruddie over his shoulder.

As the boys walked up the canal toward the city, Bird asked, "What was that lie about knowing my family?"

"I didn't lie. I think I met your grandpa up on the bluff this morning. He was kind to me and helped me. Told me that you might be on the *Minnie B. Welcome*. I'm guessing that was him and you're his kin."

"What's he look like? Old? A lot of white hair?"

"Yeah, and he carried a fancy man's walking stick, carved with a parrot's head."

"That was him, alright. That's his B&O retirement cane," replied the younger boy. "He likes to sit up there. Calls it his 'thinkin' bench.' Says he gets good ideas just sittin' and starin.'"

"He was headed down here when I last saw him."

"Yeah, but sometimes he forgets what he thinks about," sighed the boy, shaking his head.

After hiking in silence for a few minutes, Bird asked, "Have you ever been in Cumberland?"

"Nope. Never."

"Then how in the name of sweet Jesus are you going to find the doctor?"

"You still have his business card, don't you? We'll show it to someone and ask directions. How hard can it be?"

An hour later, Bird was feverish and dragging, but they had managed to hone in on the right address after mixed success in asking for directions. They stood outside of a formidable brick townhouse with white pillars gracing a portico and a set of white marble steps.

"I'm not feeling so good," said the boy. "I don't want to go in."

"Bird, your arm is broken. You've got to do something about that."

"Why are you doing all of this for me?"

"Well, I'm just trying to repay your grandpa's kindness, Bird. Besides, maybe if I help you, maybe you'll put in a good word for me with Mr. Twigg."

"Oh, sure. That's it. I knew it. You want work. And now that I'm hurt—"

"Look, I want to be friends and the master needs more help than just you with George gone. Right?"

"I guess so. But I barely kept my job. And there's no real pay in it to speak of. What do you know about canal boats and mules anyway? What's your name again? Rudder?"

"Ruddie. I know nothing about boats," answered the redhead. "But you can teach me. And I know enough about mules to know not to beat them."

With that, Ruddie put his arm around Bird and they climbed the marble steps.

CHAPTER 5

WORKING THE CANAL

Lucas Twigg returned as evening was becoming night. He was leading two mules that looked both docile and fit. The bad news was that he was unable to find an available hired hand. Those worth a damn he couldn't afford. Those he could afford were either too old or too drunk. So, he listened to Molly's suggestion that they try the boy that had befriended Bird. It was the smaller boy's idea, mentioned just before he fell into his bed of hay in the mule shed. His arm had been set and wrapped in something the doctor called plaster of paris. Somehow the story the redhead told convinced the medical man to do it for no charge. But Bird's fever had worsened to the point that Ruddie practically had to carry him most of the way back to the boat.

The Twiggs were in no frame of mind to argue about anything. They welcomed Ruddie with hardly a word, gave him a blanket and told him to find room with Bird and the mules. The sad couple then retired with little Ruthie to their cabin in the aft of the long boat, pulling curtains across the windows.

When Ruddie awoke the next morning, it was by Mr. Twigg's boot. It was still dark but the sky had started to show gray.

"Up boy, there's work to do to get away from the landing. We have to get through the lock and up to the coal yard before noon."

Ruddie was on his feet quickly, running his hands through his thatch of red hair and anxious to please his new employer.

Twigg glanced at Bird still asleep and said, "Looks like the boy is out for a while until he mends some. Leave him be. For now, you follow me and do what I tell you to do. I don't have time to teach you mule hitchin'; I'll leave that to Bird when he's able. Okay, let's get these animals over to the towpath."

That's how Ruddie's first day on the C&O Canal started. It was a dead run after that for the six hours it took them to get through the last lock and begin to load the boat's hold from the Allegheny Coal Company's cars. With Bird disabled, Mr. Twigg walked the towpath with the mules, showing Ruddie what must be done and how to do it. His lessons were in complete silence, schooling the boy with gestures, hands-on demonstrations, and the occasional foot in the rear.

Ruddie found it all new and interesting. He was used to hard work, even for a boy his age. He felt good, like he was finally doing something, even if it was just walking mules and shoveling coal. At least he was off that damn farm.

He was impressed by the Twiggs as well. The pilot was a hard man, but not like Ruddie's father. Mr. Twigg fought for his living. He worked hard. He maintained a family, strong enough to survive the death of a son. And he didn't give up. He was doing what he had to do.

Ruddie had spent no time yet with Mrs. Twigg, but she fascinated him. She was a big woman, taller than her husband and almost as thick. He watched her grapple with the tiller and expertly guide the boat away from the landing and into the long lock queue. She was not like his mother. She spent little time talking about her dreams and probably was limited in her dreaming altogether, seemingly a very practical being. And she was physically strong, unlike his mother. But he suspected that she was like his mother in a way that he could not miss—he saw her with Bird and her own little girl and Mr. Twigg. Ruddie sensed rather than knew that she had a heart and was kind, like his mother.

With the long afternoon and evening gone and night coming on, the *Minnie B.* was now riding low in dock with its load of coal. The big barge seemed to be resting, anticipating the morrow's pull down the canal. The mules were stabled, the stalls mucked out and the deck washed down. Ruddie and Bird lay sprawled in the new hay thrown into one of the empty shed stalls. The place smelled bad, but there was plenty of room for both of them. Ruddie was exhausted and his shoulders and back pained him. He lay there, wondering how long it would take for sleep to overtake his aches.

Earlier, Mrs. Twigg called him to come get his and Bird's supper which was a thick soup of onions and potatoes. It even had some kind of meat in it. Bird said it was muskrat. The soup came with a huge ear of corn on the side, so sweet it didn't need butter. That was something his mother used to say, even though he could never recall ever tasting butter.

With his arms limp and spread wide behind his head, Ruddie stared at the moon through the shed's open side. The awning-covered tiller and cabin that held the Twigg family was on the far end of the long boat, but Ruddie could still hear Molly Twigg crying softly over her lost boy.

"Mrs. Twigg seems like a nice person," he observed to Bird, lying beside him.

"Oh, she truly is. Has always been good to me, even when I didn't deserve it. I feel bad for her and Mr. Twigg. He's a good man too, although a might flinty at times."

Bird had come out of the fever by late afternoon and was feeling a little better except for his arm that hurt him something awful. He was also not sure what to do with the heavy cast wrapped around it. He kept holding it up, turning it around and looking at it with disgust.

"That doctor told me that I should come back in four to six weeks. I have to wear this thing all that time? How do I know whether it's four or six weeks? How do I know where I'll be in four or six weeks?"

"Don't ask me," answered a drowsy Ruddie.

"If I can't work, I don't get paid! You heard Mr. Twigg. I can't just sit around here for four or six weeks. "

"Mr. Twigg told me your job was going to be to teach me hitchin' and canalin'."

This got Bird's attention.

"He said that?"

"Yep, said he didn't have the time and he was going to leave it to you."

"Really!" The idea picked the boy right up. Suddenly, he felt better and his arm didn't hurt quite as much.

"Yep, but let's not start the lessons tonight, I'm dead."

"Wait, don't fall asleep yet. Tell me all you did today. We can start there."

"Bird, I'm whupped. I can't—"

"No, no, we can begin tomorrow, just tell me what you did today."

Seeing that his stable mate had his teeth into the idea of being able to impart superior knowledge, Ruddie thought it wouldn't hurt to indulge his new, wounded friend.

"Well, let's see. The first thing we did was get the two mules off and get them hitched up and out on the towpath."

"We only have two mules now." Bird was thinking aloud, mulling over what that meant. He certainly didn't have to confirm the number with the pungent beasts occupying the space right next door.

"Right, but they seem to be able to do the job. We—"

"Whoa, whoa, mule skinner, you need to know something right off. There's a big difference between two mules and four mules."

At that, Bird, despite his words and his student's state of consciousness, launched into his first lesson.

"Your typical canal boat is ninety feet long and fifteen wide. That's big enough to haul 120 tons at about three miles an hour. Fast. Two mules will do that for you, sure enough. But using four mules is the best way to go. I guess, if Mr. Twigg could have afforded the two hundred and forty dollars it would take to buy two more animals, he would have. "

"Two mules, less work. Less muck," was all Ruddie could mumble.

After sneering at Ruddie's ignorance, Bird, basking in his long experience and greater knowledge, explained.

"Look, two mules can only work six-hour shifts at a time. If you have four, you can rotate them to go longer before stopping."

"I don't mind stopping," was Ruddie's slurred response in hopes of warding off the building oration.

"You don't get it. Two mules means a lot more landings. The poor beasts have to rest and that means a longer, slower trip. More work, not less. With two, we got to keep a closer eye on the animals too. If one picks up a stone or gets sick, then it's near impossible to keep moving. We have to lock them up good at night as well. Don't trust nobody on the canal."

Bird's last bit of wisdom was lost on his redheaded student. Ruddie was asleep and dreaming about seeing the world. But it didn't stop his partner. The boy spoke to the dark thinking aloud of what all the changes meant.

The animals would now be both Bird and Ruddie's job, at least until the boat's master felt he could trust Bird with the task by himself. Ruddie would have to take over George's responsibilities as well, meaning the older boy's work would be hot, dirty, and endless. It was all about the Allegheny Coal Company because except for maybe a little flour and molasses hidden away to sell to the lock keepers they passed, that's all the *Minnie B. Welcome* carried these days. Ruddie would have to work with Mr. Twigg to load and unload the boat's dozen hatches, secure the hatches, scrub down the dusty boat with canal water and lye soap, load the hay house situated in the middle of the boat, and assist Bird whenever he could with the care of the mules. On occasion, he would have to walk the animals on the towpath when Bird was occupied elsewhere.

When the barge was moving, it would be Ruddie's job to run the race plank along the rail and man one of the long poles used to keep the craft off the embankment or other boats. Sometimes the poles would be needed to get through locks, cross the canal to the opposite side or otherwise keep them going when the mules weren't pulling. All of this was important information for Ruddie to know and he would learn it all soon enough, but tonight the lessons were lost on the sleeping boy.

CHAPTER 6

LIFE AFLOAT

Bird's new life as a teacher suited him well and he reveled in it. The young canaler was a natural, able to explain things with clarity and humor, although lessons often were delivered with a dose of mockery. This was Bird's obvious way of making up the difference in the two boys' ages and size. His spiel was not mean-spirited though and served to keep the schooling lively.

Bird's knowledge of the canal and the region as a whole was impressive for someone his age. Not only was the boy a sponge for all of the things the Twiggs had taught him, but evidently his father and grandpa had added their own barging experience to Bird's larder and steeped him in the area's rich history as well. Ruddie's lessons from the boy included getting in and out of the endless number of locks safely, use of the long poles, mule psychology, and many other things the redhead would need to do his job. On top of that, there were stories and tidbits about the towns and places they passed, places like Pigman's Ferry, The Narrows, Oldtown, the Town Creek Aqueduct, the astonishing Paw Paw Tunnel, Little Orleans, Sidling Hill, and the town of Hancock. Bird offered information on what lie ahead, as well—Williamsport, Sharpsburg, Harper's Ferry and eventually Washington, DC itself.

The young black boy frequently spoke of people as well. He talked of famous people who had haunted the area, like the young George Washington or Thomas Cresap or John Brown or a raft of Civil War generals on both sides. He passed along what his grandpa told him about powerful canal and train men like Rockefeller, Gould, and Garrett, but Bird was also full of tales about working men and women whose lives were spent along both the waterway and its parallel train tracks.

For Ruddie's part, he couldn't get enough of Bird, his raillery or his stories. Life on the C&O became fascinating and important. So, the days flew by for the former farm boy who was getting much of what had been missing in his life—purpose and a friend he could talk to.

It didn't take Bird long to realize that the cast protected his arm enough that there wasn't much he couldn't do with a little help from Ruddie. The fact that he wasn't going to get paid if he did nothing but sit around, helped in this realization. His complaining about the cast took on a new dimension though and he took to jamming a reed down in there to relieve the itching.

While there was always something to do, the boys often found themselves during the long smooth stretches with a relaxed walk behind two easy animals in the shade of the leafy, dirt towpath. Hard work would come again soon enough, so the boys were glad to take advantage of these lulls. The Twiggs found that their young hands could get things done without too much prodding and usually left them to themselves on these occasions.

This trust allowed Ruddie to begin to feel like a part of the Twigg family, including Bird. In turn, he saw his work for them not as so much as employment as it was his duty as a member of the family. He thought little about payment and only considered it when Bird mentioned it.

Ruddie felt himself getting close to the barge family, and he worried about them. It seemed that the Twiggs now carried with them a sadness that reminded him of the mules pulling the barge down the canal. And so, he looked for little ways to ease their sorrow.

"Bird, how far do you think to the next town?"

"Oh, the next big town is Williamsport and that's about twenty-five or thirty miles away. Why?"

"Maybe we could buy Mr. Twigg something, maybe some tobacco. He chews, don't he?"

"Of course he does, how many times you seen him spit? I've seen him spit all the way across the canal."

"Maybe Mrs. Twigg would like a ribbon or a bow or something."

"Where you going to get the money for those things? We ain't been paid yet."

"I'm thinkin' when we get paid."

"Well, maybe you shouldn't be counting them chickens yet. You'd better just enjoy the scenery, boy, because I'm guessing that's about all the payment we'll be seeing."

"Well, I like the Twiggs. They're like family to me."

"Yeah, me too. Say, Ruddie, I've been meanin' to ask you, ain't you got family somewhere?"

"Not anymore."

Bird had interest in family. He often spoke of his own and how he missed them. He often had a story about his father on the railroad, or he would brag about his mother's cooking, or he would laugh remembering a big celebration where everyone had gotten together, or he'd recall falling asleep to the sounds of his uncle playing the harmonica. It seemed strange to him that Ruddie never said a word about his family.

"What happened? Why don't you have people? Everybody's got somebody.

Not me. My ma and my sister, Nora, died a couple of years back.

You have a papa, don't you? Somewhere."

Ruddie had managed to put his family out of his mind for some time now. He especially avoided thinking about his father. In fact, he was building a kind of semi-belief that his father was dead and Bird's question pushed him further along that line of fiction.

"Nope. He's gone."

Ruddie hoped to be able to leave it at that. But Bird wanted to know more.

"Well, who was he? What did he do?"

Ruddie knew that once Bird started to worry that bone, he wasn't going to let go, so the redhead recalled what his mother had said and some things Nora had told him.

"He was a fireman." This seemed to make a big impression on Bird and before the boy could pester him for details, Ruddie continued.

"Well, he didn't have a badge or wear a fire helmet, but he would help them pull the hose carriages to all of the fires in the area where we lived."

Ruddie had gotten that from Nora, but what Ruddie didn't pass along from his sister was the fact that Big Russ was one of the more vicious members of the area's firehouse gangs. These men were neighborhood bullies and firehouse hangers-on whose habits were attacking and fighting other fire brigades for the privilege of putting out a fire. The only other thing Nora knew was that the family had to leave the city right after one particular big fight at a fire.

This little bit of Ruddie's history seemed to satisfy Bird for the moment, so the redhead quickly changed the subject.

"It is pretty along here. And quiet too."

"It is that, I'd say. But you never know. On the canal, you never know what's going to happen."

"Nothing going to happen right now. We're floatin' smooth as silk. All we have to worry about is stepping in one of Daisy or Clem's piles."

Ruddie knew that his simple comment would elicit a wisecrack from his partner, but he also knew it was a good way to get Bird off Ruddie's father and started on one of his own stories. That's usually all it took.

"Boy, the canal is always full of surprises, some not so good. Some you never see coming."

"You're not going to tell me about the headless ghost in the Paw Paw Tunnel again are you? I couldn't sleep that night."

"Hey, if that scared you, I'd better not tell you about the Spong family."

"Yeah, maybe you'd better not."

After a few beats that Bird waited patiently, Ruddie couldn't resist. "Okay, okay, what about the Spong family?"

"You sure you want me to ..."

"Yes! Tell me!"

"Well, the Spongs were canalers. A husband, a wife, and four kids: Thomas, John, Sam, and Sarah, I think. Sam was about your age. They were porting coal and had locked out through the river lock into the Potomac at Rock Creek, down near Georgetown. A tug had pushed them for docking up against a concrete wall just below a powerhouse. They were to unload in the morning. Captain Spong didn't see it at the time, but there was a six-inch pipe sticking out of the wall with an elbow bend that ran down into the river."

"Yeah, so what happened?"

"Oh, so you're interested now?"

Getting the look from Ruddie he wanted, Bird continued. "Around six in the morning, Mr. Spong and Thomas were getting ready to unload, putting up the hatches. Mrs. Spong was doing something down by the mule shed and the three younger kids were still asleep in bed. That's when it happened."

"That's when what happened!?" demanded Bird's agitated audience.

"That's when the power company decided to blow the boiler off."

Ruddie's eyes were like pie plates.

"Well, the pressure in the pipe was so great, that it blew the elbow right off and the steam shot straight out and through the window of the boat's cabin. In a flash, the three younger Spongs were cooked like steamed crabs."

"No!"

"Yes, sir! Never heard anything more awful in my life, except maybe what happened to George back in Cumberland. Can't imagine what Mr. and Mrs. Spong felt. Or the kids for that matter."

"That's a terrible story. You should stop telling it." Ruddie was not as happy-go-lucky as he was a few minutes earlier.

"Look, you asked me for it. Besides, I was trying to tell you that you can never relax too much on the canal. Anything can happen."

Bird's tale of woe killed the conversation and the mood as the boys trudged along the towpath. Despite George Twigg's grisly demise, Ruddie hadn't thought much about death since he left the farm. Now, those dark thoughts returned.

"Bird, you ever think about dying?"

The younger boy looked up at Ruddie and decided a smart reply would not be kind. He was wise enough and had seen enough even in his short life to see that his friend was troubled.

"My grandpa told me that there's a big wide world out here to explore and that's what I'm going to do. Dying has no part in that."

"You know what you're going to do?"

"No, I don't. I just know I'm not going to spend my life on this canal. Or thinking about dying."

"What then?"

"I don't know, Ruddie, maybe trains next. I don't have to know right now."

"Well, we don't know anything about trains and we're both too young anyway."

"Maybe you don't know anything about trains and maybe I do," replied the diminutive son and grandson of train men. Then he said, "Boy, you are making me blue now. Just because we can't have something now, doesn't mean we won't later. You have to keep trying if that's what you want to do."

"Yeah, that's what your grandpa told me."

"We Garretts are smart men."

That bit of braggadocio made Ruddie snort in derision and he bumped his hip into Bird, laughing. Stumbling, Bird laughed too as he snapped the mules' lines and called encouragement to the animals. The boys' contented mood returned with that bit of play and they continued down the shady dirt track with their whole life in front of them.

The *Minnie B. Welcome* made its way down the waterway past Hancock and Fort Frederick, across both Big Pool and Little Pool, through the Four Locks and Little Slackwater, around Miller's Bend to the C&O's halfway point—the town of Williamsport. All that way, the boys worked hard and worked together, growing close and dependent upon each other. Bird's cast grew filthier by the day but impeded him little in doing his part in the partnership. Ruddie grew a little taller and a lot stronger, but remained a boy, often deferring to the younger but more worldly-wise Bird.

At Williamsport, the barge docked near the Darby Mill, close to Lock Forty-Four in the Cushwa Basin. The animals needed rest and the barge needed supplies. Mr. Twigg was to go into town to negotiate feed prices, replace two worn shovels and a broken barge pole, buy some white paint, a new line, and purchase a few other odds and ends for the next leg of the journey down to Georgetown. Once the mules were fed and secured for the rest of the afternoon, the boys were to follow the captain into town to buy food for Mrs. Twigg. They were trusted with the cash and responsibility to acquire flour, beans, tobacco, coffee, potatoes, some leafy vegetables, and unbeknownst to Mr. Twigg, a few pieces of penny candy for themselves and Ruthie. The boys had not been paid so Ruddie's idea of gifts would have to wait.

Ruddie and Bird took off up the hill to the little burg with a sense of excitement and purpose, happy to be away from the canal and the smell of mules. As they climbed the dirt road from the basin, they could see an impressive tower rising above the town.

"What's that place, Bird?"

"Well, my Grandpa told me that's the Knights of Pythias Hall."

"Whose nights?"

"Knights, like in King Arthur and his Round Table."

"King Who and what about a round table?"

"Ruddie, I can't believe your mama didn't tell you about King Arthur, Sir Galahad and their adventures."

"No, my ma told me some things but didn't have a chance to tell me a lot of other things."

"Well, anyway, the Knights of Pythias is a group of friends who get together to do good deeds. They began about the time the war ended and they're supposed to be based upon the stories of the friendship between two guys called Damon and Pythias. And before you ask, my Grandpa didn't know any of the stories, he just heard of them."

"Friends, like you and me."

"No, Ruddie, not like you and me. If you haven't noticed, you and me, we don't look alike—different colors. The Knights of Pythias don't allow us coloreds past their front door."

"What? Why?"

"Stop asking me stupid questions now. Let's just get up this hill, find Conococheague Street, and do what we have to do."

Bird's shift in attitude from the euphoria of a boy on his own to one mad at something was a surprise to Ruddie. He wasn't entirely ignorant of the hatred and bias against blacks. He had often been exposed to tirades coming from his father. But he hadn't thought much of it or much about it, like most of what had come out of his father's mouth. Personally, Ruddie was never in a position to look down on anyone, particularly Bird, his young mentor and friend.

They crested the hill rising from the canal and emerged onto Potomac Street which held shiny new trolley tracks. Turning right at the first chance, they found Conococheague Street where they could see shops lining the avenue. The boys were drawn by the businesses they passed—a stable and blacksmith, dry goods shops, a shoe and hat store, a barber's, two hardware stores, one carrying mostly barge supplies, a newsstand, and finally a grocery store. Bird was also fascinated by the number of taverns along the street, sporting names like: The Blue Hen, The White Swan, The Golden Swan and The Spread Eagle.

Arriving at the grocery, Bird made a suggestion.

"Why don't we split up and meet back here in a few minutes. The only thing we can't get in the market is Mr. Twigg's tobacco. So, how about you get the food and because I know how to get it, I'll pick up the chew?"

"Somebody will sell you chewing tobacco?"

"Oh yeah, no problem. Give me some money."

Ruddie hesitated before turning into the market and watched his friend skip across the street and enter one of the taverns. He noticed a second later Bird come flying back out, landing on his feet, but somewhat rumpled. A large man followed, waving his arms angrily and pointing the boy further down the street to an alley next to the Spread Eagle Saloon. When the crab turned back into the bar, Bird offered a rude gesture to his back, then sprinted away in the pointed direction. Ruddie stepped up onto the wooden walkway in front of the grocery and went inside.

The redhead emerged from the store burdened with a number of bags and looked for Bird. He could have used some help even from his pal's one arm. Placed next to the grocery's front door was a long bench upon which sat a grizzled old man with one leg, his pant leg pinned back over his stump. The fossil smiled at the boy and invited him to take a load off.

Since his packages were weighing heavily, Ruddie thanked the man, sat, and rested the paper sacks of groceries between them.

"I wouldn't mind a sit, sir, I'm waiting for my friend. We work one of the canal boats, on our way to Washington, DC."

"Washington, huh? Never been there myself. Not likely to get there either," said the old man, patting the end of the missing limb.

"My name's Ruddie, Ruddie Quick. Our boat is the *Minnie B. Welcome.*"

"Well, those are fine names both for a boy and a boat. My name's Williams, Otho Williams. I'm just waiting for my own boy to finish picking up a few things in there," he replied, thumbing over his shoulder into the store.

"You lived around here long, Mr. Williams?"

"All my life, son. Before and after the war."

"The Civil War?"

"Of course, was there another war? I spent some of it right here on this bench. Hell, I can remember September 20, 1862 like it was yesterday. That was over forty years ago. I don't know how anyone who was here could forget it."

"What happened?"

"That was the night that Union general McClellan chased Jeb Stuart right down this street after the big battle over in Sharpsburg. To get away, our boys had to clear a path under the aqueduct because they had burned the bridges. The whole town was lit up by burning houses along the street due to shelling by both armies. Little Napoleon, that's what some called McClellan, never did catch Stuart who made it across the fords and back into what by then had become West Virginia."

The elder had grown animated in his retelling of the memory, pointing here and there, directing Ruddie's attention to the various locations along the street that had burned like torches. The boy was fascinated and flattered by the attention and detail the man provided. After life with his father, he was unused to adults giving him even the time of day.

"You saw all of that?"

"I sure did, boy. I was sitting right here, nursing this stump. Them blue boys took it from me at the Second Bull Run, a month or so earlier. But we showed them what for in that fight, I'll tell you."

Before the veteran could launch into his recall of the battle at Manassas, Bird emerged from an alley down the street with a small package of his own. He walked up to the bench, nodded to the old soldier and plopped down next to his buddy.

"Bird, did you get the chew?" asked Ruddie.

"Sure, I told you it would be no problem at all," answered Bird. "Did you get the candy?"

Before he could answer, the old man stood, balancing on one leg and steadying himself on the bench. With a sharp edge, he said, "Hey, boy, can't you read?"

The codger pointed to a message carved into the bench, then read it out loud: "Whites Only."

The boys looked at the sign, then looked at the old man. Bird's face had turned into a black storm front.

"You going to move me you one-legged, dying, old, white fart?" the furious little boy spat back.

"No, he won't, but I will," replied a tall, young man, emerging from the market's doorway. He was wearing a jacket, vest, high collar and tie, all topped with a stylish Hooligan cap. He was a fop but a big fop and he immediately grabbed Bird by the scruff and pitched the boy off the walkway and into the dirt of the street.

"No little black birds on the bench," sneered the twenty-something. "And if you speak to my father like that again, I'll thrash you to within an inch of your life."

Both boys were speechless, in shock. Even Bird who normally would have given back as good as he got was silenced. The threat was real and neither friend could do anything about it. Ruddie knew from experience the best thing was to get away, so he gathered the packages, helped Bird up and dragged him away.

As they crossed the trolley tracks on their way back down to the barge, Ruddie looked at Bird. He was crying, but he knew that it was anger and humiliation forcing the tears down his face, not any pain from getting thrown down so hard. The ex-farm boy knew too that he should say nothing and just be with his friend.

But Bird had other ideas. As he wiped his face with his sleeve, he snarled, "Get away from me white boy!" Then, he sprinted ahead to the canal and the *Minnie B.*

CHAPTER 7

A CRIME WAVE

That night, as always, the boys laid in the empty stall of the mule shed. Neither had spoken since they had parted earlier that day. It was Ruddie's idea to break the ice with the penny candy he bought, a surefire way to get Bird out of his funk. It was the last thing the grocer had put into one of the bags. But when they got back to the barge, the only candy in the bags was a single peppermint stick and that went to Ruthie who had been promised a treat. Evidently, the old bastard on the bench had a sweet tooth. Ruddie knew he should have been more alert and less susceptible to the old soldier's wiles. It was Bird himself who had often warned him not to trust everyone he met.

Sometime after the Twiggs had retired for the evening, Bird produced from his back pocket a half-pint bottle of clear, corn liquor which he proceeded to slug at regular intervals. This shocked and worried Ruddie. His experience with drink had not been good. Bird was a lot smaller than Big Russ Quick and the redhead knew the stuff was transforming on much bigger bodies. He vacillated on whether he should say something, wavering because he figured his friend's reaction would not help their relationship or Bird's frame of mind. In fact, Ruddie admitted that he didn't know the boy's frame of mind, maybe he could guess, but he himself had never been kicked off a bench and thrown in the dirt because of his skin color. There's no way Ruddie could know what that was like, so he continued to lay there silently, hoping his friend would fall asleep or pass out or something.

At some point Ruddie dozed off, only to awake to a moonless night and Bird vomiting over the side of the barge.

"You okay? Can I get you some water?"

"Juss leave me alone. I don't need your help," was the answer.

Ruddie watched Bird weave his way down the raceway, clutching the short rail with his one good arm, as he went. Falling against one of the barge's lockers, the boy righted himself, reached into the compartment and removed something that was obscured by the darkness. Bird then took off at a wobbly sprint over the boat's gangway, clutching whatever he had taken. By the time Ruddie shook off sleep and reacted, the younger boy had run halfway up the path to Williamsport. When Ruddie reached that same point, running as fast as he could, Bird had turned the corner at Conococheague Street.

Ruddie was gaining on his friend but as he came in sight of the shops along the dark street, he could see the slight figure of Bird bent over something in front of the grocery store. As he neared, he watched in horror as Bird reared back and pitched some sort of liquid at the Whites Only bench. When Ruddie got there, he saw that the liquid was the white paint that Mr. Twigg had bought that day. The paint covered the seat, the walkway and a good portion of the thrower as well. It was a very sloppy job due to the arm cast that now was as white as the day it was put on.

"Bird, have you gone crazy? You know what they'll do to you for that?"

"They've already done it. And I'm paying them back," the boy slurred. Then, he wound up with is good arm and hurled the still half-full can straight through the glass window of the grocery. The noise was horrendous.

"Oh, God! Now you've really done it. We gotta get out of here. Come on!" Ruddie grabbed Bird around the waist and picked him up kicking and swearing. The older boy began to run with his squirming burden back toward the canal.

The fugitives reached Potomac Street when a big man came out of one of the alleys next to The Blue Hen Tavern. He slammed into the pair, knocking them both over. Ruddie was grabbed by the shirt front and pulled up while Bird was pinned to the ground by the man's right boot.

"I saw what you two little assholes just did! I couldn't believe my eyes. These things don't happen in my town. The sheriff is going to love the pair of you."

Ruddie could smell the man's breath, reeking of alcohol.

"Get off of me, you big prick," yelled Bird.

"You'd better start showing respect for me and this town, you little black sumbitch. I'm Deputy Sheriff Miggs and you're busted. I was about to end my shift and go home, now I won't get my breakfast 'til later and the Merkels have to clean up their market and buy a new window."

Ruddie, seeing Bird once again lying in the dirt and feeling the cop's fist balled in his shirt, resurfaced the flight instincts that he used to escape his father and the farm. He slammed both fists down on Deputy Miggs' wrist, releasing his grip. He then shoved the officer as hard as he could. The man, who was supporting himself on one leg with the other on top of Bird, careened sideways and fell. The surprised deputy hit the ground hard, banging his head against one of the rails of the trolley tracks.

Bird bounced up and the boys took off running without thinking, trying to get back to the imaginary safety of the *Minnie B. Welcome*. Looking back, Ruddie saw the deputy still sprawled there, unmoving. And, as poor luck would have it, they were forced to change directions, as several working men emerged up the path from the canal. Instead of toward the water, the two found themselves fleeing in the opposite direction up Potomac Street.

Neither Ruddie nor Bird knew where they were going, other than away from the scene of the scuffle. The town was beginning to awaken and the sky was starting to show gray. As they ran, they saw no obvious places of escape or hiding and in a few blocks they slowed. Bird's face started to show a ghastly combination of panic and nausea. But Ruddie had reverted to his days on the tramp and the lessons of the mother fox. His head swiveled looking for a fence to get under or the equivalent of a sweetbriar bush. Finding none, he looked up and saw in front of them the electric trolley that used the tracks running up Potomac Street. He tried the doors but they were locked. Then he spotted the schedule card, posted on the side of the tall railcar. Ruddie was able to make out that the first time listed there was six o'clock. He didn't know it but this was The Blue Ridge Trolley, awaiting passengers who would board later that morning to begin the eight-mile run to a town called Hagerstown. The boys ran around to the rear of the car and discovered the thing's maintenance ladder to the roof. Ruddie helped Bird scramble up and they lay flat on the top, unseen by anyone on the ground.

CHAPTER 8

FUGITIVES

The trolley ride had been harrowing from the first. The car's high roof was rounded with a four-foot flat panel running down the center where the trolley's electrical connections were anchored to the car. The various parts of the apparatus provided the boys secure hand and foot holds, but they soon found that the electricity flowing down the connecting arm from the overhead power lines produced not only heat but the occasional shock. In addition, as the trolley crossed various overhead junctions, the fugitives were subjected to a shower of sparks that were more frightening than painful. The combination of breathtaking speed that produced a steady wind current and the side-to-side rocking that was natural to any train car running along track, made the ride the experience of a lifetime with no guarantee that the lifetime would be very long.

The noise of the trolley and the need to hold on precluded any talk between the boys during the trip. Lying flat, Ruddie had looked over his shoulder at Bird behind him. This friend was splayed on the roof like a water bug on the surface of the canal. His shirt and pants were torn and his feet filthy. He also wore in equal parts white paint splatter and the dirt from the Williamsport street. Of greater concern, however, was the terror written across his face as he struggled to hang on with one arm. Clearly, he was also sharing much of Ruddie's own confused mind, a racing, flood of thoughts and images of what had happened to them and what they had done.

Was Deputy Miggs alive? Had Ruddie killed him? What about the damage Bird had done to the grocery? Were they being chased? Had they gotten away? What about the canal boat? And the Twiggs? Would they ever see them again? Where were they going? How would he and Bird survive?

His last two thoughts were all too familiar to Ruddie. He had happily put those fears behind him when he had left the farm and found the *Minnie B. Wel-*

come. But now the very same dread came flooding back. Would this be the way it always would be? It was a lot for a twelve-year-old to handle.

Before long, Ruddie noticed that they had emerged from woods and farmland. Frame houses began to appear. The trolley also had crossed over several sets of train tracks which almost shook the two off the roof. Shortly thereafter, they heard the whistle of a larger train in the near distance and the railcar pulled off onto a siding and stopped.

Suddenly, an enormous, black monster, belching gray steam and cinders came hurdling right at them. The scream Ruddie heard lying on the top of the bluff outside of Cumberland split the air, much louder this time, given its proximity. With hands over his ears, the redhead looked up to see a huge, round iron plate painted with the letters "WM" about to end his life. But the thing surged past not four feet away and, with his head turned down flat on the roof, he read the words "Western Maryland Railroad" in a long blur, repeated on coal car after coal car as the train flashed by.

Ruddie looked back at Bird and expected him to reflect the same terror he felt, but the younger boy's head was up like that of a turtle. He was grinning like an idiot.

When the last of the locomotive's cars ripped by in an abrupt end to the noise and tumult, there was an opportunity for the stowaways to attempt to get off the roof. But both were so inert that the chance passed quickly and the trolley began to move again.

The city of Hagerstown emerged a few minutes later and Ruddie noticed the trolley slowing along a busy, paved street. A sign said they were on Summit Avenue and the houses they passed earlier were now replaced by runs of single-story brick buildings. The car made a right swing onto Washington Street where the low brick structures began to turn into multi-story businesses. These carried owners' names or advertised various manufacturing enterprises or offered hotel stays. A wide array of smaller storefronts under colorful, striped awnings were tucked in between or took up the lower floor of the larger structures. They were selling hardware, cigars, ladies and men's hats, patent medicines, newspapers, and much more. A host of people moved along concrete sidewalks, perhaps on their way to work in the buildings or stores. Others walked in and out of local coffee shops or sat at tables placed outside. Still others crossed the street with random purpose, dodging traffic as they went.

From his vantage point on top of the trolley, Ruddie looked down onto the roofs of the occasional automobile and into the increasing number of carriages, delivery wagons and other horse drawn conveyances that were competing for space on the busy street. The railcar's bell began to clang with regularity as it warned jaywalkers to hustle out of the way.

Soon, they slowly entered a large, bustling square. Ruddie looked up to see a gigantic Uneeda Biscuit sign perched on the roof a building, offering the snack for five cents a packet. This served to remind him that the outlaws had not eaten for some time. It also brought to mind the sad fact that they hadn't a penny between them.

These worries had little time to percolate, however. As the trolley came to a full stop in the middle of the square, the boys were spotted.

"Hey! What are you doing up there? Get down right now!" Then, with even more force: "Come here, I want to talk to you!"

This came in a bellow from a large, mustachioed man emerging from a hotel on the corner across the square. He was wearing a high crowned fedora, a pistol belt, and sporting a large badge on his chest. A cop.

The policeman's attention drew the eyes of the people disembarking from the trolley, the motorman himself, and a number of pedestrians. Ruddie's flight skills kicked in once again. He grabbed Bird's shirt, slid down the maintenance ladder and was off the car and onto the street in a flash. The two boys, keeping the trolley between them and the law, ducked down the first alley they saw.

The cop had to wait for a beer wagon, dodge two buggies, and manage to make his way around the railcar. As a result, he lost sight of the boys and stopped. That's when a couple of concerned citizens pointed him down the alley. The officer then took up the pursuit once again.

Ruddie found himself in a maze of dirt lanes and small passageways that served the rear entrances of the square's businesses. Dogs began barking and one vicious hound hurled itself at the boys until he was stopped by a stout chain. Trash cans, barrels, and empty palettes required avoiding and Bird had the presence of mind to tip a few over to slow the pursuit that they could hear not far behind.

The boys reached an alleyway that was lined with high, white-washed fences. Ruddie tried a couple of gates, found them locked and continued his sprint after each failure. A turn around a corner put them in a blind alley with about fifty feet to the end.

"Were dead, Ruddie! We're dead!" Bird was losing it.

With that, the redhead climbed a large wooden barrel against the nearest fence, hauled Bird up, grabbed his foot and, with all of his might, boosted the little boy over the fence. He could hear his friend land with a thump. Ruddie leaped up, grabbed the top of the fence, swung his foot over its edge, balanced, then vaulted over the barrier, landing hard on the other side and on top of Bird. The runaways lay there in a tangle, listening as the cop ran past the dead-end and on down the longer back lane.

"Well, what in the name of sweet Jesus is this?"

The surprised words came from a stick-like, black woman who had been interrupted as she hung wet laundry on a clothes line. All the boys could see of her was her scowling face and her ankles as she peered over what looked like a wet, white table cloth.

The boys scrambled up and stood at nervous attention, wondering if they had actually improved their situation. They knew that they had lost their pursuit for the moment, but this woman was giving them an intimidating evil eye that held them rigid.

She moved under the clothesline and confronted them, arms across her chest. Her severe expression, however, melted into complete mirth as she looked at her visitors. Hearty laughter followed as the woman bent over in pure amusement.

"You two scalawags are the saddest pair I've ever seen in this here city of Hagerstown. The cat didn't drag you in, it threw you over my fence."

"Ma'am, we're—" began Ruddie.

"And look at you, you little peanut. Half white and half black! I've never seen the likes."

At that, Ruddie looked at Bird and Bird looked at Ruddie. They both began to laugh as well. Bird's adventure with the paint can left his clothes and face splattered, one bare foot white and his hair reminiscent of his old grandpa. On top of that was Williamsport street dirt and grease from the roof of the trolley. Ruddie was not painted, but he was just as filthy from his own introduction to the canal town's street and half of his face was black with a streak of the same grease that Bird sported. Their feet looked like they belonged on wild animals.

Their amusement didn't last, however, as their predicament came flooding back.

Bird spoke first. "Ma'am were in trouble. We need some help."

"I don't know about trouble, but one thing I do know is you need a bath," answered the lady. "Now what are you doing in the backyard of the Elks Hall?"

Ruddie hesitated answering, but Bird jumped right in. "The law is after us for something we didn't do. Can you hide us?"

"Something you didn't do, huh? Why should I believe that from a couple of sad cases like you? What have you been up to? And how'd you break that arm?"

"We ain't been up to nothing really," lied Bird. "Something I said, I think. We're victims of race hate!" Ruddie nodded his head, trying to give credence to what his friend said, although he really didn't understand it.

"Race hate, huh? Him too?" she answered pointing at Ruddie. The woman didn't seem convinced by their story or their vigorous nodding. But then she said, "I guess I might know a little about that around here. What about your folks, do they know where you are?"

With a small stretch of the exact truth, Ruddie said, "We don't have any folks, ma'am. Mine are both dead and his too." The older boy put his arm across Bird's shoulder for added pathos. Then, throwing themselves on the mercy of the court, they both put the most innocent looks on their faces they could muster.

"Well, you two look like you could stand a little luck for a change. This here is the Hagerstown Benevolent and Protective Order of Elks. I just work for them, but these are good folks. They try to help those who ain't got. I'd say you boys ain't got, so I'm going to help. Come inside."

With that, the big-hearted woman ushered them into the back of the building and into the basement laundry room. There she gave them hot water and soap, left and returned shortly with two sets of clean clothes and old leather boots that had seen better days.

"You young men clean yourselves up best you can, get rid of those rags you're wearing and put these on. We got these from a recent collection the Elks had. I bet you two have never had shoes on your feet, given the looks of those dogs. Well, you're in the city now and can't go barefoot for long. These are dead men's boots and should be big and soft enough so that they don't give you blisters. I guess you're hungry too, aren't you?"

When Ruddie and Bird nodded vigorously, the woman left again and was back in a few minutes with ham sandwiches, hunks of cheese, a few gingersnaps and two glasses of milk.

The pair washed, dressed, and laughed out loud at each other's giant, booted feet. They then dug into the best meal either of them had had in a long time. Neither could believe their good fortune and, like the boys they were, began to forget the mess they were in, laughing some more at what they thought they had gotten away with. The kind woman returned to her task of hanging laundry in the yard and began to sing an old song that sounded something like "*Steal Away.*"

Suddenly, through an open window, they could hear banging on the back gate.

A deep voice yelled, "Open up, Addie, I can hear you in there. I've police business to attend to."

The woman looked over her shoulder to the basement window, then walked to the back gate.

"Who is it?" she called through the locked opening.

"It's me, Sheriff Downin, now open up, you old scarecrow."

"Sheriff Downin, you're in the Elks. You know I ain't supposed to open this gate. You and the others told me so."

"I don't care what we said, open this gate now, Addie, or you're in big trouble."

When Addie opened the portal, the sheriff pushed his way in, looking around.

"See two fugitives come through here? Two boys? One colored and one white?"

"Sheriff, you know yourself that the gate was locked. I ain't seen nothing but this laundry."

"Addie, if you want to keep your job, you'll tell me the truth."

"Now why would I lie to the law? Look around all you'd like, Sheriff."

Ruddie and Bird began to scour the room for an escape route.

"Okay, I don't have time for this. The longer I waste time here, the farther those two are getting away. They're wanted by the sheriff over in Williamsport."

It was clear that Downin and Addie knew each other and that there was little love lost between them. The laundress locked the gate behind the sheriff, took up her song again, waited a minute, then walked swiftly back into the basement.

"What have you two gotten yourself into? They're looking for you all the way over in Williamsport. I lied for you, now I want the truth!"

The boys were rattled and neither were far from tears. They were on the run; the law was still looking for them and wasn't going to give up the search. While Bird had done some damage, Ruddie had murder hanging over his head. They had no plan, no friends and no money. They were hiding in a basement and had just angered the only person who had shown them any kindness.

Bird blurted, "A man pushed me down, I got mad and I threw something through a window. Ruddie tried to save me, but he pushed a cop and—"

"Whoa, whoa, little man, calm down, take it slower, nobody's gonna get you just yet," the woman said in a placid tone. Come sit down. Then you can tell me what happened. Maybe you ought to tell it," she said, patting Ruddie on the shoulder and putting her arm around Bird and leading him to a chair.

When the boys were more settled, she said, "Okay, you can call me 'Miss Addie.' What are your names and where are you from?"

"My name's Rudyard Quick. People call me 'Ruddie.' My mother died a few years back. A couple of months ago I left a farm up around Cumberland after my father was killed in a fight." Ruddie had begun to think of his missing father in this way. "This here is my friend, Bird."

"Horatio Dewitt Clinton Garrett is my name," corrected Bird.

That raised Addie's eyebrows but she said nothing.

"Bird and I were working on the C&O for Captain Twigg on the *Minnie B. Welcome*."

"That's a canal boat?"

"It sure is, ma'am. One of the finest around. I taught Ruddie everything he knows about canaling," bragged Bird, starting to gain back some of his confidence.

"So, I assume something happened in Williamsport?"

"Yes, Miss Addie. It sure did," answered Ruddie. The boy then told her all that had happened, including his shoving of Deputy Miggs and the officer's unmoving state when they last saw him.

While Ruddie was talking and Bird had a chance to add his thoughts, Addie stood and made herself a cup of tea. She eased herself back down in the chair, tucked one leg up under the other, and took a sip of tea.

"Well, it's a fact they're looking for you but you don't know exactly what for. Maybe that Deputy was just knocked out. You said you thought he'd been drinking. I know those sheriffs and deputies stick together. And I know the sheriff who came to the back gate. He's a slimy one that's for sure and no friend to us black folk."

"What do you think we should do, Miss Addie?" asked Bird.

Addie sipped again and seemed to come to a decision. "You boys can stay here tonight. There's nothing going on in the hall until tomorrow, but you have to be out of here by mid-morning."

The relief on the two fugitives' faces was obvious, but short-lived as they both realized tomorrow would come soon enough.

"Tonight, I'll see what I can find out about a murdered deputy in Williamsport. This is a small county and there should be news in the *Morning Herald* if something like that happened. Then we'll have a better idea of the hole you dug for yourselves."

The boys were eager to know the truth of their predicament and thanked their benefactress enthusiastically.

"Don't thank me yet. Like I said, I know this Sheriff Downin and he's a hard man with a long memory. It's likely he's got friends in Williamsport too. Maybe I got a friend who can help you get out of Hagerstown without that redneck knowing. We'll see in the morning."

CHAPTER 9

THE TRAIN

The next morning came early for the boys, just as the sun was coming up. Addie woke them with a gentle shake and loomed over them as they lay on a mattress she had dragged into the laundry room for them. The woman was smiling, but her arms were crossed on her chest. Next to her stood a man wearing a US Postal Service uniform and a scowl. A small, mottled dog was at his feet. The mutt peered at the boys, turning his wiry head in a way that suggested he wasn't quite sure what they were.

"Addie, I don't believe you. You've done it again. What have I told you about taking in stray dogs? These are the mangiest yet."

"James, you're one to be talkin' about strays," said Addie, dipping her head in the dog's direction. "Plus, your life ain't so pure that you can ignore what *Proverbs* tells us: 'The generous will themselves be blessed …'"

Before she could finish, James cut her off, saying: "Addie, now you're finding them in twos, one at a time ain't enough?"

"They found me this time, James. Now you stop being rude. And you two, on your feet!"

As the boys scrambled to their feet, Addie reached for them and pulled them around to stand at attention in front of the crusty man.

"James, this is Rudyard and Horatio." She brushed at the boys and licked her hand to try to wet down Ruddie's shock of red thatch which was standing up like his head was on fire.

"Boys, this is my husband, James. He's a postman working the Western Maryland train down to Baltimore."

"Rudyard? Like Rudyard Kipling?" The man was fighting back a smile. "Well, he certainly looks like one of his jungle critters."

"James …"

"And this then must be Horatio, Hamlet's friend." James was showing off his literary side, but it was lost on Addie and the two fugitives.

"You can call me 'Bird,' sir," said the boy rubbing the cast on his arm self-consciously.

"Now, here's what James is going to do," said Addie, looking sternly at her husband. "He's going to take you two on the train with him on the morning run south. I have some church friends in Baltimore on Calvert street. They can take you in, at least for a while. We leave for the depot in a few minutes."

Ruddie found his voice. "Miss Addie, thank you for everything, but how are we going to get there without the sheriff catching us?"

This question made James uncomfortable and he shifted on his feet as he began to say something. But Addie stopped him with another look.

"Don't worry about that. I've got to drop James over to the depot in our buggy to meet the train. There's room enough to hide you two under the seat."

"Addie ..." started her husband.

"James, you know what that man, Douglass said. 'If there is no struggle, there is no progress.'"

"But—" began Ruddie.

"Look, we're doing this," Addie said forcefully. "You didn't murder anyone over in Williamsport or it would have been in the papers and I would have heard about it on the street. Also, I owe that Sheriff Downin a few things and I'm not going to let him get his hands on you."

The boys were given breakfast and a couple of paper bags full of lunch for later. Unseen by James, Addie pressed a note and a dollar bill into Ruddie's hand.

Over the redhead's surprise, she whispered, "That's the address of my friends in the city, don't lose that or the money. Don't you dare tell James where you got it."

Then they all went out the back gate of the Elks Hall. The two kids spooned together under the shay's seat and were covered with a big blanket that smelled of horse. James drove with Addie sitting next to him and the little dog squeezed between them.

Soon, they were moving across the city to Summit and Lee Streets where they'd find the Western Maryland train depot and the coal freight that was leaving for Baltimore at six o'clock. On the way, James spoke loud enough so the boys could hear him. He explained that the train did not stop as it rolled through small towns and communities. So, as a Railway Postal Clerk, it was his job to grab the mail with a catcher arm as they went by. Once one of the local canvas mail bags was aboard, James had to sort the mail before the next pick up.

As he warmed to explaining his profession, James also mentioned that it was unusual that a coal freight carried mail, a job usually done by passenger service trains. But, since the WM had not yet begun passenger service out of Hagerstown, the freight trains were doing the job. He also told them mail cars often carried the company safe and some light baggage and cargo, if there was room.

The buggy pulled into the rail yard without incident. The yardman greeted James, nodded at Addie and then directed them to the rear of the train.

"Isn't the mail car usually put right behind the steam engine? Why is it all the way in the back this morning?" asked Addie.

James could offer no explanation but turned the buggy, and eventually reaching the rear, found their destination. They would be traveling immediately in front of the caboose.

As they pulled even with the mail car and James climbed down to unlock and slide the door open, he was greeted by a trainman leaning out of the last car's door.

"Hello, Jimmy, glad to see you finally made it. I've been here since five, got coffee on the stove waiting for you."

"Barney, you need to get a life beyond that caboose. The rest of us have families and a home with real beds in them," joked James. "No coffee for me this morning, I've already had two and I have things to do before we hit the Chewsville mail grab."

"Okay, be like that," replied the trainman. "But first, let me introduce my new apprentice. They finally got me some help after all this time."

Resigned, James gave a look of caution to Addie who had taken the buggy's reins. He walked back to the caboose where a gangly young man of eighteen or nineteen stood in the doorway. He wore a dirty slouch hat, denim overalls and sported a scraggly beard that didn't look like it was really trying.

"This is Otts Purdy. Otts, this is James McLight, the best damn Postal Clerk on the W and M."

The two shook hands but neither seemed impressed. There was no exchange of pleasantries and both were happy to go back to their own business. Barney mentioned something to James about a beer once the train reached Baltimore and the men parted.

When James saw that his friend was out of sight, he slid the mail car's door open and Addie shooed the hidden boys out of the shay and up into the train. A whistle from James, and the pooch in two bounds leapt up into the opening.

Bird and Ruddie both turned to thank Miss Addie for her kindness, but James hustled them deep into the interior as their savior smiled and drove swiftly away.

The mail car was a good size but there was little space wasted. One side was crammed with trunks, travel cases, paper board boxes and a couple of large wooden crates. The rear of the car was reserved for the Postal Clerk's office. A large rack of marked pigeon holes used for sorting the mail took up most of one wall. Under it was a run of open canvas bags, each suspended on a long metal frame. A large cork board hung next to it and held schedules, index cards, and various other papers pinned to it. Opposite the mail rack was the open door that allowed for mail catches along the route and next to that was a worn chair and rolltop desk, groaning with writing tools, folders, and binders. The rear wall of the car held a small windowed door that allowed access to the caboose. Finally, one corner held an iron stove and another a squat safe on legs that was marked with a big WM. Both the stove and the safe were bolted to the floor. Several kerosene lamps swung from the ceiling.

"Boys, I need you to stay completely out of sight. The only ones supposed to be in here is me and General Sherman," said James, leaning down and scratching the dog's bristly ears.

"I'm expecting the bank courier in a few minutes, the conductor will check in after that and there's no telling who else might come by. I have to leave the door open and set the catcher arm before we leave the yards. That'll be in about ten minutes," he said, checking his pocket watch.

James moved to the baggage area and began to shove boxes out of the way. He pushed one of the crates aside enough to create a cubby hole for Bird and Ruddie. The boys climbed in behind the crate and the clerk stacked a few bags in front of it.

"I hope I don't have to tell you to be quiet. If you're caught, I'm caught. We're breaking a few rules here and I'm not normally one to do that, but I've learned to trust Addie's instincts over the years."

No sooner had James delivered his warning when a call came from outside the car. The agent from the Hagerstown Merchants Bank had arrived with a heavy canvas bag destined for Baltimore. While the man watched, the clerk took the bag, walked to the safe, spun the dial, inserted the pouch, closed the door, and re-spun the dial. James then wrote out a receipt and gave it to the courier. The man offered his thanks and took his leave, having completed his morning chore.

Ruddie and Bird had crammed into the makeshift hideaway and gotten as comfortable as possible. There was just enough light to see and each tried to read the other's face, but they had so much to say, staying quiet was impossible. Finally, Bird whispered:

"I can't believe we're on a train!"

"Shh, Bird, you heard Mr. James."

"I can't help it. I can't believe our luck. We're safe and on our way to Baltimore!"

"We ain't safe yet and shut up!"

"Okay, okay, but we're on a train!"

Ruddie gave his friend a sour look and a shove. Just then there was a squirming movement behind Ruddie and he jumped an inch or two to the side. It was enough to allow the little dog to join them, settling in on Bird's lap and looking up at the boy with the expectation of a head scratch.

"Hey, boy, hey! What do they call you, General? Sherman?" enthused Bird. "I think he likes me."

"He's the only one right now," muttered the older fugitive. "Now shut up!"

The boys' exchange was then interrupted by another call from outside the car. James moved to the door and saw the conductor coming to do the expected pre-departure check. Three other men were with him, however, and one of them was Sheriff Downin.

"Morning Chauncey, we on schedule today?" asked James.

"On the nose, James," replied the conductor. "But I got something else for you. You know Sheriff Downin, don't you?"

"We've met."

At that the sheriff, jumped in. "McLight, we have to use the Post Office's car this morning. This man is our prisoner and we've got to transport him to Baltimore for arraignment by two o'clock. Here's the paper work, signed by your supervisor."

Downin shoved the authorization at James. Being as thorough a man as he was, the postal clerk read the document through. The prisoner was Russell M. Quick caught in Hagerstown while fleeing a murder warrant in Allegany County. A background check then told Washington County authorities that their prisoner was also wanted in Baltimore for a killing four years ago that took precedence over the more recent crime.

The sheriff continued. "Deputy Matson and that Remington shotgun will be riding with you and keeping an eye on the prisoner, here. You got something in there we can chain this piece of garbage to?"

James looked at the deputy then stared at the prisoner. Matson looked serious and capable enough of using the shotgun he carried. The prisoner looked big and dangerous. Under a shock of wild red hair, he was unshaven and bruised. The man had obviously seen the worst side of life, and recently. His eyes carried heavy, drinking man's bags, but behind them were alert, black pinpoints. At present, they were drilling into James. His hands were dirty and calloused, but cuffed behind his back. He also wore a pair of heavy leg irons, lending credence to the assessment of danger.

"Sheriff, this is not what I get paid to do. I don't think—" started James.

"This is out of your hands. Your boss is the one paid to think and he signed the papers," snarled Downin. "Now where can I put this man?"

With that, the sheriff pushed past James and into the car. He and the Deputy hauled the prisoner up, looked around and decided to chain the man to the most substantial thing in the space—the safe.

The hidden boys had heard most of the exchange and now lay frightened and nervous. A minute earlier they were excited and hopeful, now they didn't know what was going to happen. There was an armed deputy riding with them! And a chained prisoner! They sat, catatonic, saying nothing and listening as hard as they could.

An hour passed that was filled with James working the postal clerk's job, catching mail as they rolled through towns and villages and sorting it before the next burg was reached. Nothing was said among the men, and all that could be heard was the loud movement of the train. General Sherman was asleep on Bird's lap and unbelievably the boy was dozing as well.

Suddenly, Ruddie heard one of the men speak. "Mailman, you keep any money in this safe?"

There was no response from James, but the voice made Ruddie jump. He would recognize it anywhere. Praying that he heard wrong, the boy quietly shifted and stretched enough to find a narrow slit between the crates and baggage that allowed a view of the other half of the car. He could see James' back, as he sorted mail. The deputy was sitting in the chair next to the side door with the shotgun across his lap. His eyes were slits. The prisoner was on the other side of the car, chained to the leg of the safe in the corner, but he was bent over studying the dial of the safe. While he couldn't see Big Russ' face, Ruddie knew him immediately and stifled a cry.

The boy slid back down into the hideaway, shaken to the core, straining to think of what to do, if anything. Looking at Bird, he wondered how his friend could sleep, and struggled with how to warn him of their situation. He was panicked and worried and wished he had never gotten on the train. The coincidence was overwhelming and it froze him physically and prevented any rational thought.

Time dragged on and Ruddie figured that they must be getting close to Baltimore. Just then, he heard a noise that sounded like someone banging on a door.

"Who's that at the rear door?" the deputy asked.

Then James answered, "Looks like Barney's new man, coming from the caboose. Maybe a message for me."

Ruddie pressed himself up to the spy hole and watched James open the rear door. As the young man, introduced as Otts, came in, he leveled some sort of big pistol at the deputy and fired. The deputy never had a chance to use his own weapon, as he slammed against the car and a big red rose bloomed on his chest. He dropped the shotgun and slid to the floor. The teenager then pointed the gun at James.

The loud report of the pistol woke Bird and the dog in a shock. The boy let out an inadvertent yell and the dog began to bark. Ruddie watched both the gunman and the prisoner look up at the crates and baggage. James had backed away against the mail rack, his arms up.

"Otts keep the gun on the mailman. Don't shoot him yet," said Big Russ. "Alright, whoever's back there, come out. Come out right now!"

Keeping his eye on James, Otts searched the deputy, found the keys to the handcuffs and freed Quick's hands. The leg irons had been welded, so Otts slid the deputy's shotgun over to the prisoner who aimed it at the chain between his legs and blew the links apart. He stood and walked over to the lawman who amazingly was still breathing. Russ Quick raised the shotgun and fired into the dying man, blowing him out of the open door of the fast-moving train.

"Otts, did you take care of the man in the caboose?" When the gunman waved the pistol to indicate he had, Big Russ said, "Good work, glad to see you made it up here in time."

Then he issued orders. "Get whoever is back in those boxes out here now. You, mailman, open that safe."

As James knelt to dial the combination, Otts climbed the pile of baggage, brandishing the pistol and threatening whoever was hidden.

Ruddie was in confusion, he had just witnessed his father murder the deputy in cold blood. Although killing a deputy was something he might have done himself, this was vastly different. The sheer violence and pure evil of it was numbing. So, Bird, holding the dog, made his way past Ruddie and out over the cargo while the redhead sat suspended in shock and terror.

"It's just a little nigger boy and a dog, Russ. What should I do with them?"

Quick was preoccupied with the bag that James had pulled from the safe, so he didn't answer. Instead, he gave out a hoot when his hand came out of it with a bound stack of large-denomination greenbacks.

"Thank you, Mr. Mailman, thank you," said Big Russ, then he swung the shotgun and slammed it into James' head, hammering him against the mail car's wall. Before he fell, the thug hit him again with the butt of the shotgun, knocking him to the floor in front of the open door. Quick then leveled the gun at James, but before he could fire, the motion of the train rolled the unconscious man out of the opening where he hit the roadbed hard, bounced, then rolled down a green embankment into a farmer's bean field.

Bird watched this with wide eyes and an open mouth, dropping the dog. The dog let out a low, menacing growl and sprang at Big Russ, sinking its teeth into the man's calf. The gunman danced in pain and fear, reaching back and trying to shake the animal off. Otts, doing his own dance to get a clear shot, fired his pistol at the dog, nearly hitting Quick.

"Christ, Otts! What are you trying to do?"

In the confusion and noise, a wild-eyed Ruddie emerged from the boxes. He ran at Otts, knocking him into the iron stove where the teen landed in a tangle of stove pipe and a cloud of ash. The redhead then ran to Bird, grabbed him around the waist, waited a beat, then leapt off the train as Bird was screaming, "No Ruddie!!"

Part II

Baltimore

Chapter 10

Arrival in Baltimore

When Ruddie opened his eyes, the first thing he saw was General Sherman. He was sitting, looking at the boy not two feet from his face. The mutt looked as if he were smiling. When the boy blinked, the dog began to wag its tail.

The next thing Ruddie noticed was the smell. Why did the animal smell so bad? It was overpowering, forcing him to sit up. This caused the beast to hop away, as the boy's movement produced an avalanche of rubbish all around him. He slid a few feet further down an embankment strewn with tin cans, paperboard scraps, parts of old wagons, broken furniture, bottles and a host of other unidentifiable trash. His skid was halted by a large, mangled barrel that looked as if it had been crushed by a giant. That's when Bird's head and shoulders emerged from underneath the thing, causing another minor landslide of debris. The bristly little dog then ran to the boy and began licking his face.

"You threw me off the train!" accused Bird, throwing a tin can at Ruddie.

They lay in a mountain of trash that had built up along the rail line right-of-way, dumped there by the neighborhood. The boys' luck held once more when they had hurtled out into thin air in a desperate bid to escape the killers. They landed on a slope of loose refuse and their downward slide had broken a fall that surely would have finished them had it been anywhere else.

"He was going to shoot us, Bird!"

"Yeah, I guess he was."

"No. He was going to kill me!"

"Probably both of us."

"No. You don't get it. My father, he was going to kill me!"

"What are you talking about, Ruddie?" Bird now started to look closer at his friend who suddenly seemed at the end of his rope.

"That was Big Russ. The prisoner was Big Russ!"

"Who?"

"My father. Bird, that was my father!"

"How in …? I thought he was dead!"

"I saw him murder that deputy and Mr. James and he was going to do the same to us!"

"Yeah, yeah, I get it," said Bird. "He's your father?"

"That's what I've been sayin'. I left the farm after he killed a man from town. I never wanted to see him again. But they caught him and he was on the train!"

"Ruddie, I hear you. But you've got to calm down. We're safe now. You saved us."

"He saw me, Bird. He knew me right away. He'll come looking for me. For us. We saw what he did!"

Bird himself was still shaken by what had taken place. He was no more used to seeing murder than Ruddie was. It was only the redhead's near hysteria that forced some measure of calm on him. He had to get Ruddie to pull it together.

"Okay, okay, that was not good, but we got away. You got us away. And we were lucky to land in this trash. Now let's get up out of here, before our luck runs out and they come looking for us. Are you alright to walk?"

When Ruddie nodded, Bird pushed the affectionate dog away and looked around. They were below the train tracks, but above a sickly looking, trickle of a stream at the base of the slope. Beyond the rail bed, rose a long line of dilapidated, brick buildings and ramshackle wooden houses.

The pair scrambled up to the tracks, causing more slides as they did. They could see a wire fence separating the rail bed from the run-down urban land-scape. The fence had been partially ripped down and lay folded over, providing an easy exit to an alley and access to the city.

Ruddie was walking stiffly and had a glazed look that worried Bird. He thought he had to get Ruddie talking to bring him back. He had to get him talking about what happened if for no other reason than to get it all out in the open. A lonely train whistle blew in the distance.

"Jesus, Ruddie! Do you think Mr. James made it? He got hit pretty hard, then fell off the train."

When Ruddie didn't respond, Bird tried another tack. "Did you know the punk you knocked into the stove? That was a neat trick!" The redhead just shook his head.

"How about General Sherman! He was great! He saved us. Sunk his teeth right into …" Then he let his comment drop as he realized he had brought his friend right back to the killer he said was his father. Then, after a few beats, he asked, "Ruddie, are you all right?"

Ruddie then shook himself and his eyes seemed to return to the present. "Bird, I hate that man. I hoped I would never see him again."

"I can see why. But we got away and we made it to Baltimore, Ruddie. That's something. Let's get out of here fast. You still have the name of the place Miss Addie gave you?"

Ruddie pulled the scrap of paper with an address on it and the dollar bill came with it, fluttering down to the paved alleyway. Bird pounced on it and stuffed it in his pocket.

"Wow, where'd you get the cash? It ain't smart dropping money on the ground in this neighborhood." Bird looked all around them.

"We have to find this address, Bird. Miss Addie said they would help us."

"Right, but I'm starving!" answered his friend. "How about you?"

It wasn't long before the boys found the city street. They were in a busy neighborhood that was distinctly down-and-out. They saw worn door fronts in narrow brick facades with long rows of marble steps in various shades of unwashed gray. They passed a variety of small stores, a ramshackle stable and smithy, a carriage repair shop, a swarthy man selling fruit from a horse drawn cart, and a clapboard building that reeked of tanning hides. In and around these enterprises, a host of people of all types, black, white, and in between went about their daily lives.

A dingy tavern seemed to be anchored on most corners, barnacled with its coterie of male hangers-on, waiting for someone or something to happen. Graying, thickset women in faded print frocks went about chores, occasionally bawling at the kids playing all over the sidewalk and in the street. A knot of older boys fought with sticks and rocks in a vacant lot while a beat cop argued with a man in an apron in front of a cigar shop. Their harsh dialogue was interrupted by a woman who screamed an obscenity from a window above them.

The three refugees jumped a thin, yellowish trickle that leaked out of alley and caught the attention of a nasty looking gang of teens who eyeballed them as they hurried past. A block later, a man swore and kicked at General Sherman as he walked past on the pavement, but then had to skip nimbly away as the dog turned and growled. Ruddie stopped to ask a man lounging on the steps of a church for the way to Calvert and Pleasant Streets. The loiterer seemed affronted by the question and hesitated in his answer. Finally, the boys were told in a surly fashion that it was a dozen or so blocks away in the direction they were headed.

As they trod on, Ruddie and Bird kept their eyes open. They were yokels from western Maryland, but no longer naïve yokels; no longer did they trust people to be honest or understanding or even civil. Too much had happened to them and the people around them. George Twigg, his parents, the Spongs, James McLight and the Hagerstown deputy—evil or bad luck had befallen them all. Even Miss Addie, as kind as she was to them, had been motivated by bad treatment from Sheriff Downin.

"Ruddie, I'm hungry," revealed Bird for the second time since they jumped from the train. Both boys had left their paper sacks of lunch from Miss Addie untouched.

As they walked, Ruddie began to come back to the moment. Something within had started to put the trauma behind him, or at least bury it deeper. Evidence of that was his appetite. "Me too, Bird. Maybe we can spend a little of our money, if it's not too much."

"How about in here, then?"

The boys had walked out of the neighborhood by the railroad tracks and into a more business-like area. They stood in front of a small restaurant called The Mount Vernon Coffee House. The place advertised its menu in white paint all over its front windows and on standup boards outside the door. There was baked hash with gravy, bread, and butter for ten cents; roast pork with peas, mashed potatoes, and butter for twenty cents; beef stew and bread for five cents; three hot cakes with butter, syrup, and coffee for ten cents; hot dogs for five cents and a lot more. Water was free one of the signs said.

"That T-bone steak with steamed beans, bread, and butter sounds really good," said Bird almost drooling. "I never had a steak before!"

"Man! That's one of the most expensive things on the menu, how about a hotdog?" replied Ruddie who felt like they needed to budget their small stake.

"C'mon you cheapskate, you've got a whole dollar. Besides, I can give General Sherman the bone when I'm finished."

"Yeah, if you don't eat the bone yourself. Okay, okay. Let's go in. I think I'll have the pork chop. It's twenty cents, but I get mashed potatoes, bread, butter, and coffee with it."

Ruddie pulled the door open and Bird barged in followed by General Sherman. There were five or six tables and only two were occupied. They sat down at one near the window and looked around for a waiter.

A pear-shaped man with a protruding abdomen appeared and looked at them skeptically. His belly pushed the stains on his apron out in front of him nearly into the faces of his seated customers. The cuffs of his white shirt were rolled, revealing thick wrists covered in black hair. The towel he carried over his arm was stained.

"What do you boys want?" was his introduction and he wasn't asking for their order. "Hey! You can't bring a dog in here! Get him out! Get him out right now!"

The waiter yanked the chair out from under Bird and moved to the door, holding it open. The boys walked back out with General Sherman and looked at each other.

"I'm hungry," whined Bird.

"Yeah, me too," agreed his friend. "General, you're going to have to stay out here."

"Aww," sounded the smaller would-be diner. But he followed Ruddie as they edged in the front door, blocking the dog as they did. It was the animal's turn to whine.

The boys took the same table and watched General Sherman sit outside the window looking in at them. The boys tried not to meet the dog's eyes. Both felt like rats, but they were hungrier than they were guilty.

The rotund waiter returned and repeated his earlier chilly greeting.

"I'll have the T-bone and fixin's," said Bird eagerly.

"The pork chop and all that other stuff for me," said Ruddie.

"Do you boys have any money?" they were asked rudely.

"Sure we do," answered Ruddie to a doubtful smirk.

Bird rummaged around in his pocket and produced the dollar and waved it so everyone in the café could see it.

The waiter sighed and asked with resignation, "How do you want your steak?"

After Bird answered "cooked" and Ruddie said "same," the man stomped away. At that, Ruddie called to his back, "And we want some of that free water too!"

A half hour later, Bird thought Ruddie looked a lot better. The two sat full and satisfied, looking out at General Sherman. The dog was waiting patiently for his companions and whatever was going to come next. The waiter brought change from the dollar, but it came up short after Bird insisted that they count it. A tip didn't even cross their mind. This didn't improve their relationship with the snot, but they didn't care. They would never see him again.

"You can't trust anyone these days," said Bird loudly, iterating one of his early lessons.

"Bird, put all of that extra bread in your pocket with the T-bone. I've got some of the chops left. We'll give it all to the General out there. What are you doing with that glass?"

"He's going to need something to drink too," replied the boy as he tucked the water glass under his shirt and made for the door.

The boys moved away from the café quickly with the dog jumping up and down and sniffing at Bird's pocket. They covered another block and were looking for a good place to stop and feed the dog when they saw an amazing sight. Rising high above the trees lining the street was a massive pillar with a statue of a man pointing at something. General Sherman was forgotten for the moment as the monument drew the two into a trot.

Soon they arrived in a huge, terraced plaza that held a massive, white marble column. The pillar was surrounded by a wrought iron fence and stood on a square building that served as its platform. The edifice was inscribed with foreign words and was made of the same gleaming material as the column. The building and column together helped push the statue on the top to an impossible height. The whole thing was so tall that the boys, standing directly below it, could not tell who it was up there.

Evidently, a brass plaque at the monument's base answered the question, but since Big Russ curtailed Ruddie's reading lessons by putting a match to his mother's books, his skill was rudimentary at best. And since Bird couldn't read at all, they asked a young woman passing by with a baby buggy.

"That's George Washington himself," she answered. "The father of our country. And, by the looks of him, the father of a lot of other people as well." Then she laughed out loud at her joke and pushed her charge on further into the plaza.

"What did she mean by that? asked Ruddie. "Why was she laughing?"

Bird looked up at the statue's silhouette against the sky and the angle of its outstretched arm and grinned. "I don't have any idea, Ruddie," he lied.

Ruddie squinted at the plaque. He could read the numbers written there. "Looks like they put him up there way back in 1829, according to this. And if I'm right, its one hundred and seventy-eight feet tall."

Then Bird cried, "Looks like there's a door, maybe there's steps to the top. Let's go!"

The boys raced to the gate in the iron fence, but found it locked to their loud disappointment. Looking around, however, they saw that the plaza was surrounded on four sides by manicured, green parks, full of smaller statues, park benches, and gurgling water fountains. Well-heeled gentlemen and ladies strolled the shady, neat paths running through this garden in the middle of the city.

Beyond the parks, on all sides, stood elegant mansions, spired churches, and imposing buildings that might have been museums or schools. Covered carriages and stylish hansom cabs vied with noisy automobiles on the cobblestoned streets surrounding the urban oasis.

Bird's mouth was open again as he took in this alien environment. The quick transition from the rough neighborhood they passed through to this opulence within only a few blocks was disorienting.

"I bet they don't have anything like this in Cumberland, Ruddie," observed the boy who had really only known the world of the C&O Canal.

The redhead was as dazzled as his buddy was.

"No, I bet they don't. I didn't expect this. It's not the Baltimore I remember when we lived here."

"You've lived in Baltimore before?" asked a surprised Bird, pushing a now very anxious and hungry General Sherman off his hip. "You didn't tell me that."

"Truth is, I don't remember much. I was just a kid. We had to leave. Let's go sit down for a minute." Bird's question had reminded Ruddie of his father.

The pair, still looking up at the president, wobbled their way over to one of the park benches along a hedge and sat, ignoring the stares from the people who passed. Bird unloaded his pockets and gave its contents to the excited dog. He then walked over to a drinking fountain and filled the purloined glass with water for the animal.

"This must be where you live if you're rich," he said sitting back down.

"Must be," replied Ruddie, looking around and not at all sure he liked it. "I don't—"

He stopped in mid-sentence, grabbed Bird by the shirt and pulled him down below the back of the bench. At his friend's complaint, he pointed, but said nothing. Bird looked over the hedge, across the park and out to the sidewalk surrounding it. There, he spotted two men walking fast. They looked as out of place as the boys did themselves. Hustling in the direction of the neighborhood along the railroad tracks were Big Russ Quick and his partner, Otts.

"Having a little picnic in my park, boys?" said an authoritative voice.

The boys turned back at the sound and jumped. Standing with his hands behind his back was a very large Baltimore City policeman. He was unmistakable in his high, round helmet marked with a laurel wreath, his knee-length blue coat holding a long line of brass buttons, an impressive shiny badge on his chest, and a long night stick hanging from his belt.

"Just passing through, I hope," he suggested to the raggedy looking pair. "By the way, that dog of yours needs to be on a leash in here."

The young fugitives were dumbstruck. They were caught and flight seemed useless in the dominating presence of this bushy-lipped giant. Neither uttered a word at first, and when Bird did, what came out seemed absurd.

"He's not my dog," the boy said.

"Not yours, huh," replied the officer. "You just like to feed stray animals T-bone steak?"

"Yes, sir. I mean, no sir. General Sherman does what he wants to do and he's been tagging along with us."

"General Sherman? That quite a name for something that size," observed the cop with what looked like a genuine smile.

Then Ruddie shook off his daze. "Please sir, we're looking for the corner of Calvert and Pleasant Streets. We're supposed to meet some people there."

A look of dawning came over the cop's face and his demeanor softened a bit more.

"I know that place. If you're looking for help, that's a good place to go. Do you know which corner of Calvert and Pleasant you're looking for?"

When the boys shook their heads, the policeman said, looking at Bird, "I think you'll be able to figure it out once you get there. Here's what you do ..."

The cop pointed them out of the park. Told them to keep going another two blocks in the direction they had been walking. There, once they got down the hill, they would find Calvert Street. Then they were to turn right, go four more blocks and they would find Pleasant.

"And take the General with you," he ordered.

The boys thanked the man and hustled out of the park, feeling the cop's eyes on their backs the whole time.

CHAPTER 11

NEW LIVES

Ruddie and Bird half-walked, half-ran down the street. Without trying to draw any more attention than necessary, they followed the policeman's directions, all the while looking over their shoulders. They hadn't really expected to see the killers again, but there they were. It seemed obvious where they were going. It also seemed plain why the they were going there. The boys were being hunted.

"If they go back to that neighborhood, there were a lot of people who saw us," said Ruddie breathlessly.

"Lots of folks out on the street. Do you think they would have noticed us?"

"Bird, think about it—a white boy with red hair, a little black kid and a scruffy mutt of a dog? Someone will remember us."

That thought didn't help their anxiety and they picked up the pace. They rushed along the pavement of a busy Calvert Street, full of horse-drawn traffic. A noisy, electric street car labeled "Blue Line" rattled by on rails running down the middle of the cobbled roadbed. They passed a firehouse, stables, hotels, restaurants, a barbershop, and a place that repaired bikes. As they drew even with an imposing church and a school with the letters L-O-Y-O-L-A carved into the stone above the door, they heard the sound of a freight train whistle. It wasn't very far away. Looking down one of the side streets to their left, they could see what looked like a large rail yard one block away. When the whistle blew for a second time, General Sherman gave a little yip, bounded across the street, under a beer wagon and darted down an alleyway toward the sound.

Bird looked crestfallen when the little beast was gone.

"I guess the General has his own things to do," suggested Ruddie. "Maybe he's looking for Mr. James."

"Yeah, maybe, if Mr. James is still alive," was the dispirited reply.

In another minute, the boys had reached Pleasant Street. They stood there in confusion. On one corner was a noisy saloon and on another a drug store with people waiting in line outside. The other two corners held a big church and across from it a building that looked like it was crowded apartments.

Ruddie suggested they try the church first, so they dodged traffic crossing the street and climbed the steps of the place. At the top, the redhead struggled to read the marquee next to the big, wooden double doors. He finally said, "Looks like a church alright. Says we can come in, I think."

Bird scoffed. "Of course it's a church, Ruddie, look at this place. It ain't no tavern." Then he asked, "How do you know we can go in?"

"If it is a church, they wouldn't have a sign out front saying 'Stay out' would they?"

Together, the two pulled open one of the heavy doors and were immediately swathed in the smell of incense and burning candles. When the door swung closed, the noisy street disappeared and they found themselves standing in near pitch black. The boys' eyes began to adjust and, looking through the vestibule into the dim nave, they could see a few scattered people sitting or kneeling in long rows of wooden benches. Several racks of little white candles flickered in the distance of the space. A woman with her head bowed slid past them, dipping her hand in a miniature fountain imbedded in the wall, then making some sort of sign on her forehead with her wet hand. The young visitors took a few tentative steps into a center aisle lined by massive columns supporting a vaulted ceiling painted with stars.

An old man sat with his head down, seemingly asleep. Several women held beads and were murmuring to themselves as they looked up at a gleaming white table on a stepped platform, lit by a battery of thick, tall candles. Over the table hung a massive crucifix with Jesus impaled upon it. Somehow he looked as if he were commiserating with those down below him, despite his suffering. Both Ruddie and Bird were familiar with the story of Jesus from their mothers, but were shocked at the stark depiction of the god who had become a man. Neither had ever been inside of a church.

To the left of Jesus stood a statue of a bearded man dressed in black and white robes. In one hand he held a tiny version of the cross, in the other a book that he seemed to be offering to the boys. On the other side of Jesus was a beautiful woman dressed in blue robes. Her head was tilted down gently and she held a kindly expression. She too seemed to be looking at the boys.

Again, the pair found themselves in an unsettling, alien environment and turned to leave. They were obviously in the wrong place. That's when a man dressed all in black except for a little collar of white and a thin embroidered scarf of some sort emerged from a small booth to their left.

"Are you here for confession, my sons?" he asked.

Ruddie started in surprise at the man's sudden appearance. He was very round and short, not much taller than Ruddie himself. His big brown face smiled out of a pumpkin-like head that balanced itself on the stiff white collar.

"What's confession, sir?" asked Bird who seemed less intimidated than his partner.

The man laughed a deep laugh as he drew closer and was able to take the measure of his visitors.

"Welcome, boys. I'm Father St. Laurent. I'm the pastor here. You're standing in Saint Francis Xavier Catholic Church for Colored People. Please come in. Have a seat." The man gestured toward a nearby bench.

"What can I do for you?"

While Ruddie gawked at the man who called himself "father", Bird said, "We're looking for friends of Miss Addie from Hagerstown. Do you know her?"

"Well now, I sure do. I was just thinking of Addie and James the other day. Did she send you to me?"

"Miss Addie said you would help us," continued the boy.

Father St. Laurent once again sized them up. Then he said, "Well, I think I can guess what help you need, but why don't you tell me."

"It's kind of a long story, sir," answered Bird.

"Is that broken arm part of the story, son?"

"It's just the beginning of the story, sir."

"Then why don't we go into my office and talk. Are you hungry? How about something to drink?"

The boys followed the priest into the parish office that was down a long hall, off the sanctuary. There, the pastor asked a woman at a desk to bring water and a few cookies. They sat in comfortable chairs around a low table and while Bird enjoyed the cookies, Ruddie told the priest their story.

At the end of it, the pastor sat and thought for a minute or two. Then he said, "I think I can help. But only to a point."

Reaching over and putting his hand on Ruddie's shoulder, he continued. "First, I'm very sad to hear that your father was involved in murder. I can't imagine what that must feel like. To see something like that. You must have been very frightened."

Ruddie had been scared and still was. He had no idea how he did what he did to get Bird and him away. He really hadn't been able to process the whole business; he had simply pushed it out of his thoughts. Ruddie preferred this priest not dwell on it. So, he said nothing and just nodded as Bird watched his face.

"It might be best to go to the police with what you've seen, but I wouldn't be surprised if you didn't want to do that, given some of the other, um, experiences you've had."

The boys were sitting up listening intently. Bird stopped eating, mainly because the cookies were gone. They both shook their heads at going to the police.

"Well then. You do know that St. Francis Xavier is a church for people of color, don't you?"

At their confused looks, he explained, "Everyone is welcome in the church, of course, and we do have a school and a small dormitory in the basement for orphaned boys. But the school and our beds are only for girls and boys like Bird here. But the demand is great and therefore can only be temporary, even for folks like us. Luckily, right now, it only needs to be temporary because we've had good luck in either placing our children or finding them jobs."

The boys heard him but still weren't completely sure of what he was saying.

The pastor, seeing that he wasn't being clear, looked directly at Ruddie, then said, "What I mean is that the school and beds are only for negroes." When both boys blinked at this, he continued quickly: "The parish council and the folks who are paying to keep the church and school going only have so much money and there are very few others who will take colored folks in."

Ruddie still wasn't getting it, but Bird was and said, "Are you telling us that I can stay here but Ruddie can't?"

"Yes, son. That's what I'm saying. You can stay but only for a while."

"Then, we're leaving. Let's go, Ruddie. Thanks for the cookies, Father."

"Whoa, whoa, son. Where will you go? What will you do?"

"I don't know, but we'll do it together. Let's go, Ruddie," Bird said again.

"Bird, I think—" started the redhead.

"Wait. Don't go yet. There may be something else I can do. If you'd like, I can speak to my friends across the street," offered the cleric, pointing in the direction of Calvert Street.

"What do you have in mind, sir?" asked Ruddie.

The priest then explained that on the opposite side of the street, the building that looked to the boys like apartments, was actually The Baltimore Boys Home and they also took in orphaned boys. Fr. St. Laurent offered to speak to the superintendent there on Ruddie's behalf.

"You mean split us up?" asked Bird shaking his head.

"Bird, wait a minute. We need help and we have to get off the street. Big Russ and Otts are looking for us. What choice do we have? We have nowhere else to go."

"We've made it this far, Ruddie."

"Bird, your friend would be right across the street. They'd find him work too. You could see him every day."

"I don't like it," said the boy.

"I don't mean to frighten you, boys, but someone needs to let you know that Baltimore isn't always the kindest of cities, especially for young men like you on your own."

This was something the travelers were learning rapidly. They listened closely to the priest as the three talked together for a little longer and it became clear that they were not going to find a better offer, at least not today. Bird was unhappy but eventually he relented. So, as the evening began to fall, Fr. St. Laurent got Bird settled with St. Francis' dormitory matron, then took Ruddie across the street to The Boys Home to try to get him located there.

As it turned out, The Boys Home was an excellent situation for Ruddie. There was space there for him as long as he didn't mind sharing a room with two other boys. They were willing to house and feed him as long as he found work, kept a job and paid a small percentage of his wages back to the home.

The redhead wasn't there a day when the work director came to Ruddie with a job working for a newspaper called *The Baltimore Sun*. The boy started early every morning, sorting and bundling papers for distribution, and stacking them in a dray. The rest of the morning was spent hawking the newspaper on the street. Once noon arrived, Ruddie went back to *The Sun's* loading dock to bundle the paper's evening edition, then he returned to the street to sell as many of those as he could. His territory was the west side of downtown, well within walking distance. The work wasn't as hard as splitting wood or working a canal boat, but his days were long and full and Ruddie was often spent by the time night came.

Bird crossed Calvert Street to visit every day at first, but soon found Ruddie gone early and asleep soon after arriving back at the home in the evening. When Bird started attending the St. Francis school at Fr. St. Laurent's urging, it wasn't long before whole weeks passed without the two boys seeing each other. When they did, it wasn't the same. Shared experience was missing. Long silences ensued after brief descriptions of what each were doing. Funny incidents weren't that funny or new adventures weren't that interesting. And when Bird mentioned the murder on the train and worried out loud once again, Ruddie got angry for his bringing it up. The boys were moving in different directions and both would just as soon forget Big Russ and Otts. Without immediate danger, the whole business began to fade with time, and the two friends were happy to let it go.

It wasn't as if they didn't like each other anymore; it was more that their separation allowed their differences to come front and center. Neither really understood or admitted their need for each other, as new lives and new friends started to take precedence over the old.

Chapter 12

The Comedienne

One Sunday afternoon when there was no newspaper to bundle or sell until Monday morning, Ruddie was in The Boy's Home common room pitching pennies. He was very good at it and his victims were two young reprobates with whom he shared a bedroom. Out of the corner of his eye he spotted Mr. Franz, the Home's superintendent, coming down the hall. Gambling was frowned upon and it did not do to annoy the man. So, to the chagrin of his two pigeons, Ruddie scooped up the change, shoved it in his pocket and stood, trying to look innocent. He was not particularly successful.

Franz entered the room, shaking his bald head. He was followed by a smiling, dignified woman. Although her dress was generally conservative, it was offset by a mass of shocking red hair that was attempting to escape out from under a huge hat. The bonnet was anything but ordinary being weighed down with what looked like a greenhouse of little red roses. As if the roses didn't provide enough flair, a fluffy pink tail of some sort hung from the back of the concoction.

"Ruddie, you like it here don't you?"

"Yes, sir, Mr. Franz," was the redhead's response.

"Well then, you'd better understand that pennies are not the only thing you're gambling when you pitch them in here. Do you get me?"

"Yes, sir, Mr. Franz."

"Now if you can refrain from taking Willie and Joe's pocket change from them, I'd like to introduce you to someone."

With that, the woman stepped forward and without waiting for Franz's introduction, said, "Hello, Ruddie. I'm Edna May Drambauer. I wanted to meet you because we redheads have to stick together."

She patted her coif and grinned in a mischievous way while Franz unconsciously ran his hand over his clean pate.

"Edna May, I mean Miss Drambauer, was responsible for getting you the job with *The Sun*, Ruddie," explained the super.

"My friends at that rag tell me you are doing quite well and I just wanted to thank you for your hard work. I like to see things work out."

Even without the compliment and thanks, Ruddie liked this woman immediately. He had not known a lot of girls or women in his life, but those he had were kind to him. This one certainly seemed an exotic bird, but he sensed she was good-hearted and even had some fun about her.

"Ruddie, Miss Drambauer is one of The Boy's Home benefactors. Do you know what that is?"

When the boy shook his head, Franz explained, "It means she tries to help our boys. Find them work, create a few opportunities. She also knows that our boys cannot stay here forever, so she tries to find them a place to live or get them settled with a family who will offer a home. Every now and then, she invites a boy or two to come live with her."

Now Ruddie was on alert. He liked The Boys Home. He like the other boys. And even though he didn't see him a lot, he liked the idea that Bird was just across the street.

Edna May saw this immediately. So, she said in a rush, "Ruddie, it's up to you. No one is forcing you to do anything you don't want to do. But I think you would find living with me has a number of good things about it. I have a nice place, uptown, a big room you could call your own and I'm a very good cook. If you wanted, you could continue to work for the paper and you could come and go as you pleased, within reason of course. And I would take good care of you until you found a place you liked better."

Before Ruddie could find a polite way to ask what he would have to do in return, the astute woman said, "I'd ask nothing of you except a little company once in a while."

All of that sounded pretty attractive to the boy, but Ruddie, like the fox kits, had grown used to his independence and couldn't imagine giving it up. Still, he was twelve and having someone to take care of him also had its appeal. He thought of his mother. It also occurred to him that recently he was feeling lonely and was missing his buddy, Bird. It might be nice to have someone else in his life.

These considerations came and went in the brief time it took to form a response. "Miss Dram ..." he began.

"Drambauer," she finished. "But I'd be just as happy with 'Edna May.' It's what everyone calls me."

"I appreciate everything you and Mr. Franz have done for me. And your offer sounds great. But I don't think I'll accept it, if that's okay."

"Why is that, Ruddie?" asked a dismayed Franz. He had a home to manage, a waiting list and a benefactor to please.

"Let the boy be, Adolf, he knows his own mind. And maybe it'll change one day. Who knows?" said Edna May smiling at Ruddie.

This lack of pressure from the woman sold Ruddie on her completely. Maybe it wouldn't be so bad, but that was still not enough to change his mind.

"It was great meeting you, Ruddie. Keep up the good work," she said. "I'll leave you my address in case you change your mind."

Then she looked at Willie and Joe and whispered to the redhead, "Never give a sucker an even break." She winked, turned in a rustle and was gone.

Edna May Drambauer was a happy woman. She had accomplished what she had set out to do almost thirty years ago. She was no spring chicken, as they say, but her age was the only thing older about her.

Her youth was spent as Klara Drambauer in the crowded, hardscrabble German and Polish neighborhoods of East Baltimore. There, she danced through the streets and her early years with an optimistic outlook and a lively temperament. It was then that she found that she loved to hear people laugh. So, although sometimes it was a matter of survival and wasn't always appreciated, she developed her sense of humor as a practical skill. To do that, she stepped outside of herself to become an exceptional reader of people—who they were, what they needed and how to give it to them, all with a twinkle in her eye.

It wasn't always easy-breezy for Edna May. When her mother and father were taken by smallpox, she was forced to feed herself and look after her younger sister, Freida. At fifteen, before the war, she was old enough to get a job shucking oysters at the Thomas Kensett cannery on Cove Street. The work was dirty, disgusting, dangerous, and required her to stand over a stinking pile of bivalves for ten hours a day. Oddly enough, the diversity of the people she met over the nine years that she did the job served her very well in what would become her future career, something she had no idea about at the time.

Klara was fired in 1867 and her position at Kensett was given to a returning veteran. This left the Drambauer girls without a means of support, since Freida claimed her constitution was too fragile to work. This setback changed nothing in Klara who maintained her sunny disposition and was secretly glad to be rid of the regular gashes from the oyster knife, her sore feet, and a back that ached constantly.

Klara, now twenty-four, responded to her bad luck by answering an ad for a charwoman at a place on Howard Street called The Auditorium. This, as it turned out, was perhaps the busiest, brightest, and most popular venue in the dazzling Howard Street Theater District. The place drew entertainment headliners from all over the world and loyal patrons from all over the East Coast, but especially from Baltimore itself. It was a place of controlled chaos, loud people, and constant music and movement. She fell in love the minute she walked in its rear entrance.

Klara scrubbed the floors of dressing rooms for exactly two weeks when the assistant of a certain well-known magician caught the flu. The illusionist took one look at her face and her figure, threw the brush she was holding into her scrub bucket and handed her an outfit that would have made her mother turn over in her grave. With that, Klara's career was launched.

For the next ten years, the ex-oyster shucker worked with most of the variety acts that graced The Auditorium's broad stage. She'd been sawed in half, held hoops for acrobatic dogs, tossed balls to jugglers, played Indians in western reviews, acted the pretty shill for countless comedians and took bit parts in all types of vaudeville, minstrel, and burlesque sketches. She began to experiment with her own comedic look or gesture and even chanced an unplanned prat fall here and there. Klara laughed through it all and made friends as she went.

Her romantic life during this time was almost as busy as her budding stage life. She saw plenty of men, some of whom she even saw more than once. Several made marriage proposals, others just proposals. Once, even a huge ring was dangled in front of her eyes. But Klara would have none of it because she was having too much fun and knew she had a lot more to do.

She was right about that too when the managing director of the theater called her into his office one afternoon at the end of a particularly successful summer run. When she walked in, another man was sitting with the director. Klara recognized him immediately as James Lawrence Kernan, the owner of half of the Howard Street Theater District, including The Auditorium, The Maryland Theater, the luxurious Kernan Hotel, and other venues. She still remembers the conversation.

The gentleman stood and extended his hand. "Miss Drambauer, it's a treat to finally meet you. I've watched you with pleasure on my stage for some time now," he said graciously.

Klara took his hand, turned on one of her bigger smiles, and said, "Thank you, Mr. Kernan. Do you need someone to be sawed in half?"

He laughed and said, "No, no. Although, that is one of your more charming talents. Please sit with us a moment."

Then he continued. "Your director and I have been discussing the upcoming fall season. It seems that our nearest rival, The Academy of Music next door, is planning on going more high-brow than they have in the past. That opens the door for us here to lockup most of the vaudeville market in the city."

Klara nodded knowingly, but really had no idea why they were talking to her.

"We think that The Auditorium needs a regular, local headliner who is identified with Baltimore, knows Baltimore and can become the face of our business. Further, we think that person could be you."

Klara was stunned. "Me?" was her surprised response.

The director picked it up from there. "Mr. Kernan's idea is that we need a beloved comedienne. A beautiful woman who can speak to our community. Someone who knows our neighborhoods and the people living in them. Someone who understands their issues—the whites, the blacks, the Jews, the Irish, Germans and Poles, Catholics, non-Catholics, feminists and anti-feminists. Everybody."

"And we need someone who can make them laugh while she's doing it," added Kernan.

That was the day Miss Edna May was born. Miss Edna May the irreverent, voluptuous, bawdy, beloved standup comedienne. In the ensuing twenty years, Edna May Drambauer built that love for her joke by joke, gesture by gesture, issue by issue. With it, came both wealth and celebrity. With those two assets came valuable contacts and friends, people who otherwise may never have had the pleasure of knowing the ex-shucker from Highlandtown. And the beauty of it all was that now Edna May was in a position to give back to the city she loved. That was why she was a happy woman.

CHAPTER 13

THE NEWSBOY

Ruddie continued to be satisfied staying at The Boys Home and working for the *Baltimore Sun*. He worked the streets and corners downtown within a triangle formed by Lombard, Charles, and Liberty Streets. Each newsboy at *The Sun* had his own territory and infringing upon that of another just was not done. But that didn't mean he worked the streets alone.

The city was large enough to support several newspapers and *The Sun's* chief rival was the venerable *Baltimore News American*. The paper was another daily that used the broadsheet format and could trace its roots back into the 1700s, well before that of *The Sun's* 1837 founding. True and acrimonious competitors, the two fought for news, readers, and power for years, waging war in Annapolis, city hall, and on the streets. As ongoing proof, the owners maintained a pair of impressive buildings that squared-off across narrow South Street, throwing punches at each other with huge billboards that screamed headlines, opinions, and scoops.

Ruddie learned about the rivalry the first day he hawked a newspaper. Cuffed around and chased off one of his prime corners by bigger *News American* newsies, he was forced to adopt a new set of survival skills. Again, the foxes' training came in handy. It wasn't long before he knew his competitors' patterns, found ways to beat them to the punch, developed a cadre of regular readers, and knew every potential hiding place in a ten-block radius. He had always been fast on his feet, but now he also had become cunning and tricky.

The redhead added one more asset to his arsenal of skills the day after he found his cache of papers torn up and scattered down an alley. He bought a Colt model folding pocket knife and learned how to use it.

Even with the skirmishes that became almost daily routine, Ruddie thrived in the job. His territory became his turf and he knew how to use it to his best advantage. He built a following among his on-the-way-to-work regulars, shopkeepers appreciated his punctual deliveries, and barbershops full of men knew his name.

Ruddie even developed a distinct call that the area's denizens came to recognize. So, when Roosevelt acquired rights to build the Panama Canal, when Orville Wright flew, when Boston beat Pittsburgh in something new called the "World Series," the redhead sang out, urging people to read all about it. All of this resulted in increased sales and better tips, not to mention respect from his competitors. He had become an urban fox.

Only once did he feel compelled to use the knife. It happened on a cold December morning over on Liberty Street. He was exiting one of his regular stops, a barbershop, after unloading several papers and pocketing a couple of nice gratuities. He had about five issues left before he would have to pick up more from one of his hidden stores. Ruddie stepped outside and pulled up the lamb's wool collar of a warm coat he bought at discount from one of his regular stops. He spent all that he had saved from weeks of tips, but he was glad he had, now that the Baltimore weather turned raw.

Just as the shop's door closed behind him, he was confronted by a group of older boys.

"Look at the newsboy with his fancy coat," the largest of the gang said.

"Goes with his pretty red hair," said another.

"I wonder where he stole it," said a third.

"It's cold out here. I want it," said a fourth.

"Then take it, Smitty," said the biggest boy, slapping down with his fist and knocking the papers out of Ruddie's hand where they began to blow all over the street.

When the pack had backed him up against the shop's red and white pole, the redhead moved fast. He yanked the knife out of his back pocket, grabbed the big boy's shirt front and pulled him close. The blade came up under the bully's chin, and was held there. The others froze.

At that, a man in a suit came out of the barbershop.

"Having a little problem, Ruddie?" he asked.

The newsboy said nothing, focused on his adversary's wide eyes, but he knew the man to be Thomas P. O'Donnell, a detective with the Baltimore City Police.

"Maybe you'd better put that tooth away, before someone gets hurt," he said.

Ruddie backed away then, still holding the blade, shaking with an animal intensity.

"Go on boys, beat it, before I have to call the cops," the detective said.

"Come on, let's get out of here. He's just a punk," said one of the gang.

With that, the group slunk off, looking at Ruddie over their shoulders.

As the redhead watched them depart, he looked beyond the group. Evidently, their leader had hung back and emerged from a doorway, as the gang reached him. He was an older teenager and bent to say something to the biggest boy in the group. Then he looked back at Ruddie.

"You okay, Ruddie?" asked O'Donnell, patting him on the back.

"Yeah," the boy answered. But he wasn't. He was rattled to his core. The teenager with the gang was Otts Purdy.

That night, he went looking for Bird over at St. Francis. But he was told that the boy was not there, out with a friend.

All of the fears that came out of that ride on the train came flooding back for Ruddie. Somehow, he had managed to forget it, to focus on the life he was building. He told himself that his father wouldn't bother trying to find him in this huge city. Now, he felt like the city wasn't big enough.

There was no mistaking Otts Purdy and Otts clearly recognized him. It didn't help that he heard O'Donnell mention his name, the name Bird had screamed when they jumped from the mail car. So now, it was a just a matter of time before Big Russ learned of Ruddie and where he could be found. What would happen after that, he didn't want to think about.

Since living in Baltimore for a little while, Ruddie had learned something of its neighborhoods. He now knew that the area that he and Bird had landed in when they arrived was called Biddle Street, in one of the northeast wards. Friends at the paper also told him that the area was the birthplace of the most vicious of the old firehouse gangs, the Plug Uglies. It was a name hard to forget and one Ruddie remembered from his early days in the city, before the farm. It was the neighborhood of Big Russ Quick. It was the neighborhood he and Purdy were headed to that first day.

That night and for several nights after, Ruddie had trouble sleeping regardless of how tired he was. He was also worried when he was out on the street during the day, being cautious about everything and everyone around him. There was no longer joy in what he was doing and that was beginning to be noticed and reflected in sagging sales.

Travels to and from his territory and trips to *The Sun's* Iron Building on South Street became sprints and more than once he had the distinct feeling he was being followed. Ruddie took to turning corners quickly, then backing against a wall, or watching behind him in the reflection of windows, or searching faces in crowds. He stopped using his distinctive sales call and often turned in fright when someone stopped him to buy a paper. He never saw his father or Otts but he felt them nonetheless.

It was also frustrating that he couldn't connect with Bird. His buddy had jumped at the chance to go to school and was evidently taking it very seriously. Ruddie was told more than once that Bird was unavailable for that reason. His friend had also taken to the work he had found down on the City Dock and The Basin which kept him busy when he wasn't in the St. Francis classroom.

One evening, Ruddie returned to The Boys Home later than he usually did. At the end of a very long, cold day, he had been called in to explain his recent drop in sales to his circulation manager. The boy also wanted to avoid Mr. Franz who was looking for him regarding his late "rent." So, he entered the building through a little-used side door into the boiler room that he had scouted out when he first arrived at the home.

Ruddie made it to his room without being seen, but when he got there, he found his younger roommate, Willie, sitting on his bed, crying. Joe had moved on a week or so earlier and Ruddie knew the two were close, so he assumed that was Willie's problem. But as soon as the redhead walked in, Willie jumped up and ran to him.

"Where have you been? Are you all right?"

"I'm fine," replied a mystified Ruddie. "Why wouldn't I be?"

"There was man here. Looking for you. A very scary man. Mean. Said he would be back."

Ruddie stood very still.

"He threw me down when I told him I didn't know where you were or when you'd be back. He didn't believe me and he wouldn't leave."

"Where is he?" Ruddie managed to squeak out.

"I don't know. He ran out and down the back stairs when Mr. Franz was coming down the hall. Ruddie, who was he?"

Without answering, Ruddie moved to the window that overlooked Calvert Street. His vantage point from the third floor allowed him to see all four corners where Pleasant crossed the busier street. Although the winter evening had turned dark by that time, the boy could see a number of men standing outside the well-lit saloon on the southeast corner. He wasn't sure, but either of two dark figures standing by themselves in the shadows could be his father.

Ruddie hadn't accumulated very much during his stay in The Boys Home, so it didn't take him long to pack his duffle. He searched briefly for the address left for him by Miss Edna May Drambauer and found it in a dresser drawer.

Then, putting a couple of dollars on the dresser, he said to Willie, "Give this to Mr. Franz, tell him that I had to go. Tell him thanks for everything. Tell him exactly what happened tonight and that, if you ever see that man again, call the police."

"But, Ruddie—"

"See ya, Willie. Don't pitch pennies."

With that, Ruddie was out of the room and down the hall. He avoided the front door and suspected that someone may be watching the back exit as well. So, he worked his way down to the boiler room and slipped out the same way he came in.

Chapter 14

The Student

Bird's frustration with not being able to connect with Ruddie both figuratively and literally was gradually eclipsed by developments in his own life. At St. Francis, he found not only a father and mentor in Father St. Laurent but a community in which for the first time in his short life he felt like he belonged. Father St. Laurent even had the cast on his arm removed. As he got to know the priest and the other boys living there, he discovered shared experiences that he could never have had with Ruddie. Not that he wasn't attached to his redheaded friend in strong ways, and what they had gone through together could never be forgotten, but Ruddie would never be able to live in Bird's skin. To see what he saw, to feel what he felt. It was about race and it was about how the world treated those who were not like themselves. Bird feared that he would never be able to bridge the gap between he and Ruddie. Not that this friend ever seemed to notice the differences between them, but Bird could and did. There was never a need for explanation among his new friends, they all lived the experience of men's hatred and prejudice, even when it wasn't overt or intended. It was still there. And it was the mutual experience at this level that Bird had missed and was now providing some comfort.

So, when the two friends began to drift apart, the extraordinary effort it would take to close the gap that was now so clearly identified for Bird was too much. Calvert Street became more and more difficult to cross, and Ruddie's own life wasn't making it any easier. In addition, Bird discovered that he loved school and loved the world it opened for him. He was learning to read and write, he was learning the perspective of history beyond life along the C&O Canal, he was learning the languages that would allow him to take advantage of his natural intelligence. He was developing a sense of himself, some confidence beyond what too often in the past had been just bluster and whistling through the graveyard.

On top of all of this, he had work that he liked. The woman Edna May, who had helped him to get it, was a mystery to him in large part. She was someone he hadn't even imagined could exist. She was a white woman, certainly, and couldn't fully understand, but somehow she overcame that difference between them by something that only could be called love. Love for people, love for he and Ruddie.

Edna May had arrived at St. Francis one afternoon and sat in the back of Bird's reading class. He had been called on to read a paragraph he had written as an assignment. The boy had chosen to write about a local hero—the fighter Joe Gans. He read his scrawl haltingly from the front of the room.

"Joe Gans is a great, champion boxer. He is from Baltimore and they call him the 'Old Master.' I like him because he is little but tough, like me. I'd write some more, but I can't think of a good punchline."

When Bird looked up at the class with a huge grin on his face, Edna May laughed out loud. That did it for her. She had to meet this young comedian. So, after class, she asked Fr. St. Laurent if he would introduce them.

"Where'd you get that sense of humor, young man? I loved your joke and I was hoping I could borrow it from you."

"Bird, this is Miss Drambauer, she helps us here at St. Francis. She also tells jokes for a living," explained the priest. "Edna May, this is Horatio Dewitt Clinton Garrett, better known as 'Bird.'"

With a grin of her own, Edna May said, "You know, I knew a pirate boxer once who had a mean left hook."

That did it for Bird. He stuck out his hand and said, "Pleased to meet you, mind if I borrow your joke?"

The two were immediate friends and Edna May asked if they could chat for a while, so Fr. St. Laurent invited them into his office. She was interested in who Bird was and how he came to live at St. Francis. As the priest explained, he mentioned a second boy who had arrived with Bird who was now across the street in The Boys Home.

"Ruddie Quick," Bird clarified.

"You're friends with Ruddie?" she asked, surprised.

"Sure, he's my best friend. How do you know him?"

Once Edna May explained, the commonality solidified the obvious chemistry between the two jokers. After that, their conversation was easy and fun. As Edna May made to leave, Bird asked her how someone got a job telling jokes.

"Bird wants to find work as well as go to school," explained the priest.

"Well, now, seeing that you're interested, I'll show you. Father, do you think it would be alright if I took Bird to lunch one day, give him a tour of The Auditorium?"

The priest thought that was a fine idea and Bird looked delighted, so plans were made.

On her way out, she said, "Bird, I'm not sure I can get you work telling jokes, but I do know some folks who are pretty good at finding jobs. Maybe we'll have lunch with them. Okay?"

Edna May and Bird hit it off famously. Bird didn't mind the attention at all and the comedienne gave him plenty of it. Her reward was the look on his face as they walked into the theater, when they went backstage, when he sat in the seats to watch a few acts rehearse, and when she gave him a preview of her own act (cleaned up). But the most fun she had was when they walked across the street to The Diamond Cafe.

Hours before, she had made it plain that she wanted him to call her Edna May. He tried but the best he could do was "Miss Edna." She settled for that.

"Miss Edna, are you sure they'll let me in here?" he asked standing outside the tavern. "The last time I walked into a bar, they picked me up and threw me out."

Amused, Edna May looked at the boy and said, "That's a story you'll have to tell me some time. But don't worry about it. I know the owners. Come on."

She grabbed his sleeve and tugged him up to the front door and through the double stained glass doors. Once inside, the two stood at the top of the carpeted steps that led into the main taproom. Most of the tables were full of folks eating lunch before returning to work. It was a noisy eclectic crowd of men, women, suits and overalls. No one seemed to care about anything but their waiters and their lunch. The long bar was only half full and there were two seats available next to a pair of black men sipping on beers. One wore an apron, the other a three piece suit.

With an intimidated Bird in hand, Edna May walked right over to the empty seats and asked, "Pardon me, gentlemen, but are these two seats taken?"

Both men turned, then stood. The man in the apron said, "Edna May that seat is yours whenever you want it, whether someone's in it or not." Then he gave her the hug of two old friends.

The second man said, "Edna May, I've missed you. And I have a bone to pick with you too—"

Before he could finish, the comedienne said, "Now, Joe, that joke went over huge and I heard you loved it." Then they hugged as well.

Edna May turned to introduce Bird and saw that he was in a state of shock, his mouth hanging open. Holding in a laugh, she said, "Bird, I want to introduce a couple of old pals. This distinguished chef is Moss Tilghman of the Eastern Shore Tilghmans and this hard case is Joe Gans, you may have already heard of him.

Bird was practically comatose but managed to stick out his hand in response to Gans' gesture of greeting.

"I thought you might like to meet Mr. Gans and I wanted you to meet Moss as well. Let's get some lunch." Then she practically hoisted him up onto one of the stools. As they sat, a big burly bartender walked over with a wide smile.

"Well, what'll it be Edna May? It's unusual to see you in civilian clothes."

"Wilbert, you have to get out more," she said with a laugh. "Let me introduce you to Horatio Dewitt Clinton Garrett, better known as Bird. Bird, this is Wilbert Robinson the catcher for the Baltimore Orioles and the tavern's owner. I'm not sure which comes first."

Robinson gave her a crooked grin and asked, "Are you of the Mt. Vernon Garretts?"

Bird finally found his voice. "I don't think so, sir."

Then Moss suggested that Bird try the tavern's hamburger and asked if Edna May wanted her usual, a gin and tonic with fresh lime. She nodded her thanks and reached for the bowl of pretzels on the bar.

The boxer moved over next to Bird when the seat next to him vacated and started to chat with the boy as he took in the surroundings and devoured the hamburger when it arrived.

"Moss, thanks for asking Joe in, I think Bird is thrilled."

"Good. I'm glad, it was nothing, the 'Old Master' loves kids. Now, what else can I do? You say he wants to find work?"

"Yeah, but he's also in school and I don't want to stop that. He's a proud little guy so the job has to be real, but maybe something that will let him do both?"

"Okay, I might have something. It's doing some cleaning and supplying of boats for a friend down on City Dock. Just maintenance stuff really, maybe stocking supplies before a sail. I'll talk to him see what he likes."

It was the best day of Bird's life up to that point. The theater, Joe Gans, a professional baseball player, a hamburger and maybe a job. It didn't get any better than that.

CHAPTER 15

RAGS TO RICHES TO RAGS

All Ruddie knew is that he had to run. But where? St. Francis was too close and maybe Big Russ knew about Bird as well. That left one place to go. He looked again at the note from Miss Edna May: One East Chase Street, Suite Five. Ruddie knew that Chase Street was a few blocks north of the plaza that held the Washington Monument. But he didn't quite know what a "suite" was. Maybe her home was among the posh places he and Bird saw when they first arrived in Baltimore. She seemed to be a well-to-do lady to him, but he wasn't really sure about what that should look like.

He eventually found Chase and was surprised how busy it was for a Monday night in December. In fact, the whole area was busy. He watched couples bundled in top coats and furs walking briskly by him and expensive carriages go past, one after another, creating a line of traffic. They all seemed to be headed west on Chase Street toward a large building ablaze with light.

Checking the addresses, Ruddie realized that the crowd's destination was, in fact, One East Chase Street. He stood invisibly across from the building and watched a steady crowd climb a long set of white marble stairs, walk past a battery of liveried doormen and enter the ornate stone archway. On first look, he imagined a castle, right in the heart of Baltimore. The place had to be over twelve stories high, soaring over any of the other structures around it. The main entrance was flanked by four enormous, carved columns that supported a massive pediment grandly etched with the name: Hotel Belvedere.

Ruddie read the address on Miss Edna May's note one more time just to be sure. He tried to smooth his hair down, brushed at the front of his winter coat, hefted his duffle bag, took a deep breath, and crossed the street to the entrance. He fell in behind an elegant couple who were climbing the marble steps. Almost immediately, he was accosted by one of the doormen.

"Pardon me, sir, may I see your invitation?"

"Invitation?"

"Yes, sir. Tonight is the Grand Opening Dinner Party for the Belvedere's special guests."

"I'm here to see someone."

"Yes, sir, I'm sure you are. But you still need an invitation."

"But—"

"No invitation, no entry. Now, beat it sonny!" The man was too busy to continue his polite charade with some kid.

Ruddie backed down the staircase and drifted off to the curb in front of the place. His adversary was soon absorbed in welcoming another party to the event. The boy thought about trying to dart past this sentry, but saw that there were others stationed up by the door. If he were to get in, it would have to be through guile.

The redhead waited for a group to disgorge from a huge brougham that had just pulled up. They were absorbed in themselves, chatting noisily and excited to see the newest and grandest hotel in the city. Ruddie ducked in among the women who were dressed to the nines in heavy furs and busy, layered gowns. As the top-hatted gentlemen in the party dealt with the doorman, he slipped by unnoticed and reached the entrance. The doormen there were so concerned about assisting the ladies through the huge set of revolving doors that again, tucked in among the frills, he went unseen.

Once inside, it was easy to go undetected. A crowd jammed the vestibule, shedding and checking coats and hats before entering the main lobby area. The noise was deafening, as the energized throng greeted friends and acquaintances there for the party.

Avoiding the cavernous lobby decorated for Christmas, its impressive, marble reception desk and the cluster of staff surrounding it, Ruddie moved with the crowd and wondered how he was going to find Suite Five. He heard a shrill-voiced woman explain to her companion that the banquet and ball rooms were situated on the top floor. That must mean that living quarters were somewhere in between. He looked around and spotted a handsome staircase across the wide room, but getting there would be a problem. He was being swept along in a river of Baltimore's upper crust, flowing toward a bank of elevators.

Ruddie had never been on an elevator and wasn't sure he wanted to go on one now. Regardless, he was propelled by the horde and eventually compressed into the corner of one of the things. He rode the box for what seemed like forever in an intense cloud of chatter and lilac perfume. The stout woman in front of him who didn't even realize there was a boy with a duffle bag between her and the wall, took forever to get off the car. So, he eventually emerged a bit breathless and dizzy.

The redhead found himself in a grand reception hallway that served as the connector between the banquet hall and the main ballroom. It was decorated lavishly for the holidays in white and gold above rich oak paneling. The area was broad enough to disperse the crowd and many of the guests had already moved into the banquet hall. Others stood in small groups conversing before going in to dinner.

With the herd now thinned, Ruddie was not so anonymous and he began to get stares and comments from the swank guests. He noticed one tuxedoed gentleman walk over to a member of the hotel staff and point in his direction.

His task now was to find the down staircase. He was not getting back on that elevator. As he looked around, he discovered a resplendent Miss Edna May not far away, laughing with a distinguished gentleman dressed in formal attire. Ruddie was about to walk over to her when a hand fell on his shoulder.

"May I help you, son?" a man asked. His brass name plate showed that he was a Mr. McCahan, manager of the hotel.

"Yes, sir," said Ruddie. "I'm looking for Miss Edna May."

At that, Edna May looked up from her conversation and registered real surprise. She excused herself and hurried over.

"Ruddie, how nice to see you. You have chosen an interesting night to visit me. Is everything alright?" she asked with concern. She noticed the bag he was carrying.

"No, ma'am, I need to talk you," he admitted.

"Okay, we can do that. Can it wait until after dinner? I have some people I need to talk to myself tonight."

When Ruddie hesitated, Edna May said to the manager, "William, may I ask you to show Mr. Quick down to my suite? I'd appreciate it if you would get him settled in the back bedroom as well. Maybe get him something to eat?"

"Of course, Edna May. It would be my pleasure," replied the manager.

With that, Ruddie was checked into the Hotel Belvedere, Suite Five.

When Edna May arrived back in her rooms that evening, she found her guest sound asleep. So, she let him be and allowed the urgent matter to wait until morning.

Ruddie woke a little later than he usually did and wandered out of the bedroom into a sumptuous room that was lit by huge windows, looking out over Baltimore's rooftops. Tastefully decorated and furnished, the space had been cleverly broken up with levels and faux walls into a large living room, a kitchen, a dining area, and a small library. Off the main room was a larger bedroom opposite the one he had used and a generous bathroom between.

Drawn by the smell of food, he found Edna May sitting in the dining room enjoying a second cup of coffee. Breakfast was keeping warm in silver serving dishes on a sideboard.

"Good morning, Ruddie. Would you like some breakfast? There's orange juice, eggs, bacon, and cinnamon rolls. Help yourself."

"Thank you, ma'am," he responded and began to investigate the offering.

"Did the bed suit you? Did you sleep well?"

"I guess so, ma'am, but I'm not used to such nice things."

"The bed at The Boy's Home wasn't as soft?" she teased.

"No, and neither was the mule shed that Bird and I used to sleep in."

Edna May laughed at that and then with a grin said, "By the way, I met this Bird of yours. Quite the fellow. Horatio and I had lunch together recently."

"You know Bird?" asked Ruddie, fully surprised.

"Yes, I do. I met him at St. Francis. I'm one of the sponsors of their school too. But we can talk about that later. I'm concerned about you. What brought you to me from the home last night?"

"Well, ma'am, it's a long story ..." he started.

"Ruddie, if we're going to be friends, I'd like you to call me Edna May. Now eat, and when you're finished you can tell me the story."

After breakfast, the two sat and talked for a good while. Edna May was quiet letting Ruddie get it all out. She only asked one or two questions and uttered the occasional "tsk" and the odd "oh!" When Ruddie told her about his father, she gasped and sat down next to him.

When it looked like he had no more to tell her, she said, "Ruddie, I don't know how to tell you how sad this all is and how sorry I am that you're going through it. I am very glad that you have come to me. I want to help in any way I can."

Then Edna May said, "Well, first things first. You can't go back to The Boys Home and probably not your job until you are safe from this man, Quick. Second, we need to warn Bird as soon as possible and be sure he's safe as well. I'll take care of that this morning."

"How are we going to be safe from Big Russ and Otts?"

"I'm not sure yet, but I have a few friends in town that may be of help. You remember that man I was talking to last night in the hotel?"

"Sort of."

"Well that man was Robert McLane. He's the Mayor of Baltimore City and he can do a lot of things."

"But I can't talk to the cops. What about the trouble in Williamsport?"

"Ruddie, I think we can get to the bottom of that. I doubt that you killed anyone and if we have to pay for a bench and window, then we will. Give me a chance to get that ironed out. More importantly, there's a couple of murderers out there and they're looking for you."

After that discussion, Edna May spent time at her writing desk since she had not yet acquired a telephone. Instead, she sent notes out through the hotel staff. The woman got dressed to go out around mid-morning, begged Ruddie to stay put, and left, promising to be back before evening.

That afternoon was as long a day as Ruddie could remember. He paced the suite from one end to the other like a caged animal. There was nothing to do except worry. He spent a good portion of it staring out the windows across tarred rooftops and past church spires, down to The Basin and the harbor. He knew almost immediately that, as kind a person as Edna May seemed to be, he could never live with her in this place. The suite was starting to give him the same feeling of claustrophobia that the elevator had the night before. The sense grew to such intensity that he began to think that life on the street dodging danger might be preferable.

When Edna May returned, she had a surprise for him. She had gathered up Bird and brought him with her. When the ex-canalers saw each other, they were delighted and showed it in the way of boys by pushing and shoving each other around the suite.

Ruddie's spirits were lifted instantly and began asking his friend a barrage of questions about the same time Bird was doing likewise. It took Edna May and the cake she brought with her to bring enough calm to the reunion that she could tell them what she had done that afternoon.

Her first note had gone to Fr. St. Laurent to be sure Bird was under protection. Her second went to her friend Mayor McLane at his home on West Preston Street, asking him for a few minutes of his time on an urgent matter. Then she set off to meet with both men.

Once the Mayor understood the situation, he moved quickly. He used a telephone to call Police Commissioner Upsher who was very interested to learn that Russell Quick and Otts Purdy were back in Baltimore hiding out, maybe up on Biddle Street. The Commissioner was already aware that Quick had escaped when being transported for arraignment for a 1902 murder in Baltimore. He also knew that Quick and Purdy were suspected of the murder of a railroad employee and a Hagerstown deputy sheriff during their escape. What he didn't know was that there were two witnesses to the crimes. As a result, detectives would be assigned forthwith to interview the witnesses, track down the criminals, and bring them to justice.

The Mayor also asked the Commissioner to look into a possible incident in Williamsport involving the death of a deputy there this past fall. By the end of the day, the Mayor was told there had been no such death of a deputy and the closest incident they had to that was the firing of a Deputy Miggs for drinking on duty.

Edna May had one final bit of news from Fr. St. Laurent. He had written to his friend in Hagerstown, Addie McLight, to tell her that the boys had come to him and that they were both well. Addie responded with great relief to hear that Bird and Ruddie were okay. She also explained that James had been hurt badly that day, but now was recovering.

All of this news was of course met with glee by the boys. But Edna May cautioned them both that they were in danger as long as Ruddie's father and Otts were still at large. She suggested that the two friends remain with her until they had assurances that the threat had passed.

Bird accepted her offer immediately and grinned as he looked around at his good fortune. Ruddie was not as enthusiastic, however, he realized that perhaps now was not the time to consider alternatives. Edna May, astute reader of people, saw the boy's reticence right away and assured him that the arrangement was only temporary. While she urged him to stay, she took pains to tell him that he was still free to go whenever he wanted to.

It wasn't long before Edna May made ready to go out again. She was on at The Auditorium that evening at eight. She ordered dinner for them from the hotel and explained that they could share the back bedroom that night. She would be returning late and they were not to wait up for her.

That night, Ruddie and Bird lay side by side in the hotel's big soft bed.

"Boy, did we ever get lucky! Isn't this great? My Grandpa would drop his teeth if he saw me now!" Bird had never imagined his situation in his wildest dreams.

"It's okay," answered the redhead. "You can't see the stars or the moon." Ruddie was thinking about happy nights in the mule shed.

"Ruddie, what's wrong with you? You don't know a good thing even when it's all around you."

"Why do you think Edna May's being so nice to us?"

"Don't tell me you don't trust her, Ruddie, after all she's done for us?"

"It's not that. We'd be in big trouble without her help. But I don't know, it's like she's trying to tame us or something."

"Tame us? She can tame me all she wants. Do you know what she did the other day? She took me to her work, The Auditorium Theater! Showed me the stage and all around, even performed a little of her act for me. Then she took me to a place called The Diamond. I met Joe Gans! The real Joe Gans! And a big-league baseball player. I had a great big juicy hamburger and pickled eggs at the bar. I even talked to the chef. He got me a job down on the water. I never even knew this stuff existed before Miss Edna May, Ruddie!"

"Yeah, she's nice. I'm not saying she isn't. It's just that I liked it when it was just us. You and me."

"Ruddie, we were on the run, scared, broke, and hungry. Now we're none of those things for the first time ever. I'm in school. I'm learning to read and write. I thought you were okay. I thought you were doing really well with the newspapers. I know you've been busy as hell."

"Maybe I'll go back to that. I don't know."

"Well you can't go back to that yet. It wouldn't be healthy."

"I can't stay here, Bird."

Bird was quiet for a few minutes, then said, "No, I can't stay here forever either. Edna May is nice and all, but she's not me."

"What's that mean?"

"She's not colored. She doesn't understand. Miss Addie understood. Fr. St. Laurent understands. That chef I met, Moss, he really understands. You don't even understand."

"What! Who knows you better than I do?" asked Ruddie.

Bird was quiet then and Ruddie was feeling a bit wounded. Bird was his best friend in the world. Maybe "was" is accurate, the boy thought. They had drifted apart ever since they had come to Baltimore. The two seemed to be looking for different things. Ruddie wanted his freedom. What did Bird want? His own kind? Whatever that was. Maybe just family. Maybe both.

Ruddie and Bird stayed with Edna May through Christmas and into the new year. She made sure that the holidays were the best they had ever had. That wasn't too hard to do, but the soft-hearted woman seemed to be filling a gap in her own life. All of the hotel's amenities were theirs; she showered them with gifts, fed them grandly, and she took them safely to holiday shows and events. They even had a Christmas tree that they decorated together.

Edna May also made future plans for them once the threat had passed. She arranged further schooling for a willing Bird and tried to do the same for Ruddie. When the redhead rejected the idea, she worked it out with her friend the mayor to find the boy a job. Through all of this, Bird seemed happy and content for the time being. Then, one day, Ruddie was gone.

CHAPTER 16

THE BURROW

When Ruddie left Edna May and Bird, he couldn't avoid feeling just the way he did when he fled the farm. He wasn't sure where he was going, but staying was worse than leaving. The actress had been kind to him and that was different. And Bird was his friend, that was different too. But shedding the sense that he was being chained up, caged, was exactly the same. So, he went, sorry that he was leaving those who had been good to him, but exultant that he was free and on his own. Free to a point—he hadn't forgotten about Big Russ.

The boy had forgotten, however, how difficult the trek through the woods and over the mountain had been and how lonely and hungry he had become. But some of that came back in force as he walked the cold, raw streets of Baltimore in January. Eventually, he found himself returning to his newspaper territory where he knew the lay of the land. He had to go to ground somewhere, find shelter, a place where he could safely hide and stay warm. The killers scared him, and maybe they knew where he might be, but Ruddie was confident he could avoid them, if he had to. How much longer could the two elude capture anyway?

There were several places Ruddie used to stow his papers out of the weather and away from *News American* newsboys. Some were even inside buildings, unbeknownst to owners and watchmen. One in particular he knew had a relatively warm, little-used basement. It also had a way in and out that was easy and fast. That spot was the John E. Hurst and Company building on the south side of West German Street between Liberty and Hopkins Place.

Hurst was a wholesale distributor of dry goods and notions. The company used the basement of the six-story structure to store merchandise, awaiting the summer sales across the southern United States. Ruddie knew that he could push open a barred, basement window because of a rusted latch, then reattach it in a way that it looked undisturbed. Inside was a huge warren of crates, paperboard boxes, and other kinds of packing cases that filled the room to capacity. The space was wired for electricity, but dim natural light filtered in through a series of glass deadlights embedded in the sidewalk around the building. They provided a degree of visibility without drawing the attention that turning on electric lights would. Ruddie also surmised that company staff were not likely to visit the basement with any regularity until spring. So, the shivering redhead headed to the Hurst Building.

Deep in among the crates Ruddie built a comfortable and compact nest from opened boxes of blankets, coverlets, cushions and other household dry goods. From among the notions sold by Hurst, the boy borrowed a low table, a small cabinet and metal locker to store things. He added a small kerosene lamp that he was careful to keep an eye on, given the flammability of his surroundings.

Once his retreat was livable, Ruddie cautiously walked the several blocks to *The Baltimore Sun* on South Street. His idea was to somehow regain his job and territory and to pick up where he had left off almost a month earlier. Unfortunately, he had been replaced by another and there were no other openings available. He was told that he could buy as many papers as he wanted and sell them as he could, but not on his former turf. This was not an option since he didn't want to spend what little money he had left and he didn't want to be too far away from his bolt hole. Ruddie even tried crossing the street to *The News American* but their district manager remembered him as a successful competitor and refused to talk to him.

Forced to extend his job search outside of the Liberty Street area, the redhead looked for work along City Dock and in the produce businesses rimming The Basin. He offered to bus tables in the Pratt Street oyster houses and restaurants in the neighborhood they were calling Little Italy. The bakeries and delis in Jewtown had nothing for him either. So, after each disappointing day, Ruddie returned to his hideaway both desperate and hungry.

Finally, with reluctance, the boy made his way over to City Hall on Holliday Street to try to see Mayor McLane about the job that Edna May had attempted to arrange for him. There, the mayor's gatekeepers were more alert than those at the Hotel Belvedere and no amount of cunning could get him past either the guards or the long line of people trying to see the man. Two nervous days of standing outside the huge domed building waiting for McLane to come out were fruitless, as well.

Ruddie might have invested another day waiting except that the longer he stayed in one place, the greater the risk that Big Russ or Otts would spot him. He knew this was a risk but it still came as a shock when he looked across the wide plaza in front of City Hall and saw his father walking in his direction, looking from side to side. Some instinct told him to stand stock still, not to draw attention to himself. But something more primal told him to run. When he did, Russ Quick looked up just in time to notice the panicked boy and the chase was on.

The redhead bolted up Baltimore Street, but as he did, he was grabbed by the sleeve of his coat and spun around. The sleeve ripped and Ruddie fell free into a clutch of empty garbage cans set out on the sidewalk. He had run right into Otts Purdy who had been closing on the plaza from the opposite direction from Quick.

Ruddie scrambled up and ran blindly into the street right into the side of a slow moving horse pulling a buggy. The horse reared in surprise, but in doing so blocked Ott's second attempt to grab the boy. By that time, Big Russ had closed on the other side of the skittering animal, but Ruddie jumped up on the buggy's long step as the horse and driver started to pull away. One more grab by Otts and Ruddie's sleeve tore down to the elbow, but the horse had jumped the contraption far enough ahead that the boy now had a few yards head start on his attackers. He used it to duck in among a knot of men congregating in the plaza, then darted behind a hot dog vendor's cart, bounded toward a hedge surrounding the open space and threw himself over it.

That was enough zigging and zagging that his two pursuers lost sight of him, so he crawled along the base of the hedge, until he watched the two thugs pound away in the direction of the tall, brick Shot Tower.

When he was sure they were gone, the boy crawled out, crying quietly and trying to pull the sleeve of his coat back up on his arm. That was far to close a call. The thought occurred to him to return to Miss Edna May and safety, but instead he headed back to the Hurst Building at a run.

Without money to buy food, Ruddie was forced out of hiding again and reduced to visiting the immense market on Lexington Street. The place was always busy and crammed with a collection of counters, stalls and display cases that sold anything anyone could want. Food was its specialty, however, and he found pilfering a meal surprisingly easy for someone with his skills. Pinching dinner was a snap, until the day he got caught that is.

Ruddie had a can of Maryland Chief tomatoes under his shirt and a small white potato pie about to join it when he was chased by the pie's irate baker. The foxy boy darted around a corner stall and ran right into an enormous chest covered with a blood-splattered apron that smelled of fish and carried the words Faidley's Seafood on it.

"Tony, I think the rats in here are getting thinner," the chest said to the arriving baker.

The huge man had a fist full of Ruddie's hair and the thief wasn't going anywhere.

"Yeah, this is the first red one I've seen though. Where's that useless house dick we hired to do the exterminating?" said the plaintiff in the affair, snatching back his wares.

"Please, mister, let me go," begged the redhead in pain. "I'm just hungry." Then the can of tomatoes fell out from under his shirt.

"I can see that, boy. Ever think about working for your supper instead of stealing it?"

"Jobs are hard to come by, sir. I'd work if I could."

"Is that so?" replied the man that smelled like yesterday's bluefish. "Well then, come along. I've got something for you to do."

The man transferred his fist from Ruddie's hair to his arm and pulled him over to a busy stall that was surrounded on all sides by long trays of iced fish, oysters, eels, clams, mussels and a host of other Chesapeake gifts. He pushed his captive through a door in the cubicle and locked it behind them. There was no escape.

The placed reeked in a way that forced Ruddie to pinch his nose. Two other men in bloody aprons stood in the big stall gutting and dressing a mound of fish, throwing the entrails into a metal bin. Not all of the mess made it into the receptacle.

"What's your name, boy?" asked the fishman.

"Ruddie, sir."

"Of course it is. Ruddie, your punishment for trying to steal food from the mouths of my friend Tony's babies, is to pick up whatever doesn't make it into the bin and wash the floor down. When the bin's full, I'll get somebody to help you carry it out back. Then do it all over again."

Ruddie looked around one more time for a means of escape.

"I'll tell you what," continued the man. "If you do a good job, I'll even pay you. Not much, you hear, but enough to feed yourself anyway."

That was enough for Ruddie. No cops. A job. Food. He nodded in thanks as much as submission. The boy was now in the seafood business.

As the new year, 1904, turned into February, Baltimore's weather turned vicious. It snowed in fits and starts, but the temperature hovered around that point that tends to produce freezing rain. Each morning Ruddie rose from his snug hideaway and hustled the four or five icy blocks to the Lexington Market. His work at Faidley's was disgusting, but it was paid work and his diet improved considerably. Mrs. Faidley even repaired the arm on his coat. When the day was done, the boy returned to the Hurst Building, slipped inside and most nights was asleep not long after eating whatever he had brought with him or whatever was left in his little locker.

This existence went on for about two weeks when it happened. It was a Sunday morning and the market was closed. Ruddie had just emerged from a cocoon of blankets and lit the kerosene lamp against the dark, gray day outside the building. He was wondering if it was worth leaving to find breakfast when he thought he heard a noise. Keeping quiet, he waited to see if was his imagination, but then he heard a distinct slam. He could tell that the sound did not come from over by the elevator to the upper floors or over by the stairs either.

The boy now was sure that there was someone else in the basement. The intruder was groping his way through the murky labyrinth and getting closer. Ruddie had a main path through the maze of crates from the window to his nest, but he also had been wise enough to build a back exit out of the refuge that essentially was a narrow tunnel under the big boxes. This was hidden behind his locker.

Afraid of making noise that would draw the trespasser to him, Ruddie sat still. Too late did he think to douse the lamp.

Suddenly, looming up over a crate was Big Russ Quick. Seeing that he had run his quarry to ground, the killer grinned.

"Well! There you are, Ruddie. You're a hard little bugger to find. I've been looking all over for you. You've always been a slippery little snot."

Ruddie said nothing, frozen in total fear. He could smell the booze on the man.

Quick, holding a long knife low and behind his leg, moved quickly to block the entrance to the hideaway.

"Have you missed your ole daddy? It was a real surprise to see you on that train. You didn't even stay to say hello." Big Russ' humor was lost on the boy.

"A little bird told me about your hidey hole and the window, so I thought I'd come see it for myself. And here you are." His voice was laden with syrupy menace.

"Speaking of birds, that runty black friend of yours is done too. Otts has taken care of him."

With that, the cutthroat leapt at Ruddie, blade coming up level and stabbing. The boy squirmed away into a corner, then rolled quickly to avoid the slashing edge, as Big Russ followed with a downward hack. The redhead's dodge saved him but took him away from his hidden means of escape.

Hampered by the small space, Quick swore and lunged again, but Ruddie scrambled away once more. As the boy was about to lose this deadly game of tag, he had managed to position the small, metal locker between him and his attacker. Laying on his back, Ruddie shoved the locker as hard as he could with both feet. The box slammed into the man's shins, taking his feet out from under him. Big Russ fell hard on his face, the knife gouging the palm of his hand. That gave Ruddie the chance he needed and he dove into the hidden opening.

Quick was not slow and he sprang after his quarry. But the killer was a big man and was only able get half way into the tunnel. He managed to grab Ruddie's ankle with a bloody paw, but his knife hand was pinned back behind him. The panicked boy kicked wildly at his father's grip while the assailant pulled and twisted mightily trying to back out of the narrow shaft with his fugitive in tow.

What the assassin didn't know, however, is that he had kicked over the burning lamp on the table as he attempted to free himself. Once he realized what he had done, his own panic set in. He dropped Ruddie's ankle and, in abject alarm, he felt flames begin to lick at his feet as the kerosene began to ignite everything it touched.

Drunk and on fire, terror took over the big man. In a frenzy, he attempted to force the crates around him to allow him to stand up. This had the immediate effect of an avalanche of heavy packing cases that pinned him to the floor. Big

Russ began to scream as he felt himself being devoured by the bonfire around him.

Once free, the boy flew to the exit window, ignoring his father's dying shrieks. He yanked a heavy blanket from a half-opened carton and climbed out. When the window swung shut, the burning man's wails ceased, but they continued to ring in Ruddie's ears as he ran away as fast as he could.

CHAPTER 17

THE FIRE

What happened after his escape from the Hurst Building was mostly a blur to Ruddie. It was no blur, however, to the city, its five hundred thousand people or the brave firefighters from all over surrounding states that fought the raging blaze for over thirty hours. Mysteriously started in the basement of the John E. Hurst Company, and driven by a twelve-mile per hour wind, the inferno burned out the heart of a great city. It swallowed seventy blocks, turning fifteen hundred buildings and lumber yards and over twenty-five hundred businesses into piles of rubble.

Ruddie did recall certain vivid details, snippets that were seared into his memory in a way that could not be forgotten. Drawn back to the Hurst Building by the clanging of fire bells and the running of people, the blanket-wrapped boy stood among a growing crowd outside the building. He remembered watching the Number Fifteen Engine Company break down the company's door on German Street. He watched as thick black smoke poured out of the opening and heard a loud "whoosh" as flames immediately shot upward. He will never forget the deafening explosion caused by the back draft. Nor will he be able to erase the memory of the terrified crowd as the explosion hurled fire brands among them and into the windows of neighboring buildings no more than thirty or forty feet across the narrow street. He watched an engine get crushed by a collapsing wall and a giant horse drag another huge piece of equipment away to safety. He saw harried firemen manning hoses whose streams only reached to the third floor and were diffused at that by thick ice forming on the overhead telephone and electrical wires. These things would be with him for a lifetime.

Even with the most calamitous event of his young life unfolding before him, Ruddie stood there with the appalled spectators and thought mostly about Bird. Shivering as much from shock as the cold, the redhead recalled Big Russ' exact words: "Otts has taken care of him."

Bird is dead? How could that be? Wasn't he with Edna May? Wasn't he safe?

Before long, the fire and the cold drove everyone away, many began to run in order to try to save whatever they could from their own homes and businesses. Over most of the next two days, Ruddie wandered the streets, lost, seeking whatever shelter he could, trying to stay warm. He was forced steadily north out of the path of the devouring flames. His old newspaper territory was completely gone, now a landscape of some terrible nether world.

The boy made his way to the market, but found it closed tight and surrounded by its stall and shop keepers who were preparing for the worst while hoping the fire stayed south of them. With his options dwindling, Ruddie walked east through streets full of firemen and fire equipment. National Guardsmen and cops were also on every corner, on alert to prevent looting. His destination was The Boys Home which he found buzzing with activity. Both the home and St. Francis across the street were taking in as many homeless children as they could. The Boys Home had been converted to a dormitory with mattresses filling every available space. There, Ruddie found a place to lie down and stay warm.

At some point, the redhead rose and walked across Calvert street to try to talk to Fr. St. Laurent. The priest was close to his emotional limit when Ruddie asked him about Bird, only to find out that he hadn't been seen since he had left with Edna May weeks before.

The Boys Home was not only a refuge, it was a source of news. The fire had taken the buildings of four of the city's major newspapers, including the *News American* and *The Sun*. Reports at first were scarce, but intrepid editors like Mencken of *The Herald*, remained mobile, moving with the blaze and issuing dispatches through the telegraph and the telephone to publishers outside the city. The delay that using external publishing caused didn't stop news from circulating, however. Places like The Boys Home became hubs for whatever information was available, both accurate and inaccurate.

Through their informal network, The Home's residents heard that firefighters had finally gotten the blaze under control a mere four blocks south on Fayette Street. They also learned that the flames had rampaged east all the way to the Jones Falls stream. Below that, terrible damage had been done to the central business district and the docks, the wind-driven inferno only halted by the water of The Basin.

Stories of heroics and intense drama emerged. Reports began to go around about the young mayor's disastrous decision to blow up buildings to create fire breaks. At the same time, other stories circulated about his unrelenting dedication to fighting the enemy. Amazingly, it was said that no one had yet lost their life in the fire. This bit of news became something of a source of civic pride for the devastated city and it was a lift for those hearing it in The Boys Home.

Ruddie, however, didn't feel it or believe it. He knew of at least one who had died in the fire in the Hurst Building. He had also been told by Fr. St. Laurent that, in fact, the body of a black man or boy had been found on Bowley's Wharf among the burned out docks. Ruddie translated this tidbit, mere rumor or not, to mean Bird. This pushed the redhead into a place he had never been, even during the years on the farm. His world, as he had imagined it, had become very dark. It had come crashing down all around him and now he was completely alone.

CHAPTER 18

THE GUARDIAN ANGEL

A day or so after the fire was finally out, Baltimore, despite smelling like the bottom of a dirty hearth, began to shake itself alive. The Boys Home too began its return to normalcy in trying to place the boys filling its hallways. In that effort, the exhausted Mr. Franz noticed Ruddie among his many charges. The boy wasn't easily recognized because he wasn't the same boy the director had come to know. His lethargy was alarming and it worried Franz, so he sent a message to Edna May Drambauer at The Belvedere. Within the hour, Edna May was at the front door.

Ruddie offered no resistance as he was bundled into a carriage and driven back to the hotel's Suite Five. The next couple of days saw a doctor come and go, but no major injuries or illnesses were found. The physician, however, did come away describing a severe "depression of spirit."

Edna May took it very slowly with Ruddie, not forcing any conversation or activity. She made him as comfortable as she could and responded to anything he might want, although his wants were practically nonexistent.

The actress was now in the first retirement of her life and was glad to have the time to help her charge. The Auditorium was being torn down and rebuilt, to reopen as a venue for moving pictures in September. The stage she had dominated for so many years was to be no longer and Miss Edna May was now Klara Drambauer once again.

Sensing no positive progress in Ruddie's will or energy, the actress attempted to break through the boy's apathy. As he stared out of the window at the portion of the city they had started to call "The Burnt District," she came to him with a letter.

"Ruddie, I got a letter from Bird today."

Edna May got no reaction from that. It was as if he didn't hear her.

"He tells me that he's settling in very nicely, but he misses you and me."

At that, Ruddie's head came slowly up. His face held a look of distrust, maybe even anger that she was making a very bad joke. Edna May ignored his expression and pressed on.

"He wishes he had had a chance to talk to you before he left."

"Stop! Bird is dead! I know he's dead, don't try to fool me. I know he's dead!"

Edna May was shocked, not only by the boy's reaction but also by the vehemence of it.

"Ruddie, what are you talking about? Bird's not dead."

"Yes, he is! I know it!" Ruddie yelled. The redhead began a wracking, uncontrollable sob, born of grief, injustice and loneliness.

It frightened Edna May and she went to him and put her arms around him. He tried to shrug her off but she persisted and drew him down onto the sofa and held the shaking boy, until he gave up and let his head drop onto her shoulder.

Edna May held him and, after a while, said gently, "Ruddie, I would never lie to you. Bird is alive. This is his letter to me. Look at the date. His writing is a little shaky but that's only because it's new to him."

"How do you know, Miss Edna? Tell me." Ruddie leaned away from her then, looking at her face with tears running down his own.

"Ruddie, a lot has happened since you left us. An opportunity came up for Bird that was too good for him to ignore. We didn't know where you were. Believe me, your friend is alive and well. And happy as far as I can tell."

"Where is he? How did—"

"You and I have a lot to talk about, but I don't want to force you to do that if you don't want to. You should know by now that all I want to do is make you as happy as Bird is. Do you understand?"

Ruddie nodded and wiped his face on his sleeve. After a minute, he began to talk to Edna May. He started telling her about where he's been, what he had been doing and what had happened to him. In the process, he painted a vivid picture of life on the street and unconsciously illustrated his own skill in adapting to it. When he got to that terrible Sunday morning, he hesitated and began to break down again.

Edna May saw it and slowed him down, urging deep breaths and asking if he wanted to stop. But Ruddie was made of sterner stuff, got over the hump and continued. He shocked her like she had never been shocked before when he described the scene in the Hurst building with Big Russ. But his benefactress had to stand and walk away with her hand over her mouth when she heard the facts of how the Great Baltimore Fire really got started.

Now, it was Edna May's turn to cry. For the first time in her life perhaps she didn't know what to say, what to do, or how to react in any way. She started to say something several times and stopped each time. Finally, she sat down again and took Ruddie's hands in hers.

"Child, I can't imagine what you've been through. I want to do anything I can to help you get over all of this." She continued. "First, despite what that awful man said, Bird was not harmed. Quick's accomplice, the boy Otts, was killed in a gun battle when the police tried to take him into custody. That happened the Saturday night before the fire. You can consider him completely out of your life. I will tell you all about Bird when the time is right, just not now, okay? Believe me, he is doing well.

"Next," said Edna May, hesitating while trying to be as gentle as she could, "your father is dead. Good. He is gone and we don't have to worry about him anymore either. If you can, let all of those fears go. They are over.

"Finally, I don't know what to do about the fire. I need to talk to friends I can trust. I suspect it may not serve anyone to learn the truth, but that's just me. Why don't we let that worry just be for now, okay?"

When Ruddie nodded, she asked one last question. "Do you think it would be okay if you stayed with me for a little while? Not forever, just a little while."

Again, the boy nodded and this time he wasn't feeling trapped.

Ruddie seemed better after learning of Bird and unburdening with Edna May. There remained something of a cloud over his head for some time afterwards, though, simply because of the magnitude of the trauma he had been through.

Edna May, being as smart as she was, knew that it would take time and maybe distraction as well for Ruddie to forget. In her experience, most children adapted quite well and this child already had a lot of experience doing that. The woman was tireless in her thinking and was already kicking around an idea that might just do the trick.

CHAPTER 19

MOSS

One afternoon, there was a knock on the door of Suite Five and when Edna May answered it, she was joined in the living room by Moss Tilghman. His hair was as white as Bird's Grandpa's and his manner was as gentle but that's where the similarity ended. When he reached for Ruddie's hand in greeting, he had an air of intelligence and strength. Edna May gave him a sincere hug and it was clear to Ruddie from their smiles that they were old and close friends.

"Ruddie, I want you to meet a special friend of mine. This is Moss Tilghman of The Diamond Cafe and advisor to the rich and powerful. Thankfully, he has deigned to chat with us average Baltimoreans today." With that, she gave her visitor a playful wink.

Tilghman laughed and said, "Son, I hope by now you've learned that Edna May is a big tease. And that's why we love her."

Ruddie was a little surprised by the adults' banter, but it wasn't off-putting and the man, while dignified, also seemed comfortable and friendly.

"Ruddie, I've asked Mr. Tilghman to come talk to us about your experience with the fire. He can also tell you more about Bird and what he's doing. Why don't we come sit down and have some of my iced tea?"

As they were getting comfortable, the man said, "I hope you'll call me "Moss" and I can call you "Ruddie.""

The boy nodded but said nothing more, not used to being asked if he could be called what he had been called his whole life.

"I've asked Moss to come today because if anyone can advise us about what we should do, it's him. He knows the city and the people who run it better than most and is in a position to help if he can."

"Why don't you tell me the story, Ruddie," Moss said. "Do you think you can do that now?"

"Yes, sir, Mr. Moss," said the boy.

"Moss."

"Yes, sir, huh, Moss."

With that the redhead let the story unfold. Again, he was clear and forthright. And again, the story was chilling. Moss listened without interruption and paused before commenting.

"A couple of things before we talk about what we should do next …" His use of "we" was a strong signal that Moss was prepared to help his friend and her charge. "Ruddie, I can tell you without a doubt that Bird is alive and doing well, but more about that in a minute. Despite reports, I happen to know that city officials are aware that there were two people who died as a direct result of the fire. Thankfully, no firemen, at least not from the fire itself, but they know of a man who got trapped on Bowley's Wharf as he tried to save the boat he was working on. Why they've kept it quiet speaks to a desire to maintain the city's image despite the fact that half the city is in ashes. But maybe most infuriating is the fact that he was a black man, and to some, inconsequential, whether he was involved in a heroic act or not."

Moss looked at Edna May with a scowl, knowing she understood very well what he was saying. Ruddie wasn't so sure.

After another pause, the man continued. "I also know that they found the remains of a body in the Hurst Building debris, although they had no idea who it was. You have solved that particular mystery. Again, they have kept it quiet for the sake of appearances." It was likely that Edna May had let Moss know that Quick was Ruddie's father. If she had, he had chosen not to mention it now.

"Be that as it may, we need to let the police know that it was Russell Quick for two reasons. First, they can stop using scarce resources looking for him. And, second, we need to tell them they can stop looking for you, Ruddie, their only witness to the murders on the W&M train."

"But Bird was there too."

"Yes, I know," said Moss, "but when the police talked to him, he told them he saw James McLight get hit, then tumble from the train, but never actually saw any murders. That's why the police need you."

"But if we tell them about my …" Here, Ruddie hesitated, but then went on. "… father, we'll have to tell them about me in the building. It was my lamp that started the fire!"

"Ruddie, maybe you shouldn't have been in the building, but you didn't kick over the lamp," said Edna May. "Besides, you were just trying to get away."

"I think Edna May is right, Ruddie. My advice is that we go to the police with the story. It's up to them what they do with the information. I don't think you have anything to worry about."

"Moss, I'd like to talk to Robert McLane about this too," added Edna May. "I want him to know because of an idea I have."

"I don't see a problem there, if you can get to him. He's the busiest man in the city right now."

"Oh, I think between us, we can steal a few minutes of the mayor's time."

When Moss nodded, she suggested he let Ruddie know about Bird.

"Ruddie, Bird is with very good friends of mine, family really, over across the bay in Crisfield. Have you heard of the place?"

When the boy shook his head, Moss explained, "Edna May introduced Bird to me some weeks ago. He's quite the character, isn't he? Well, we got to talking and I asked him what he wanted to do when he was older. He really wasn't sure, so I asked him what he liked. He told me that he liked school and being around water. He also said he loved food and that someday he wanted to work on the railroad."

Ruddie smiled because if he had been asked what Bird liked, except for school, that is exactly what he would have guessed Bird would say.

"Well, I started to think about that and in talking to Edna May, we realized that it may be a good thing to get him out of the city. Quick and Purdy were still out there and Bird was no longer useful to the police for the reason I mentioned. So, I contacted my friends, the Swanns. This is a family that owns a great restaurant right on the dock in Crisfield. That's a town on the Tangier Sound of the Chesapeake. These folks took me in when I needed help and they taught me how to cook in wonderful ways. They lost their own boy a few years back. I thought the situation perfect for your friend. The Swanns did too."

"Bird really liked the idea," said Edna May. "When I talked to him about it, he mentioned the water and the food and the chance to learn something new. But what I think sold him was the fact that he would be with the Swann family. I'm guessing he misses his own folks."

Ruddie was quiet while the two adults explained Bird's decision. He was glad for him, but sad for himself. His friend was gone. But Ruddie knew deep down that he and Bird were different and probably wanted different things. Ruddie knew himself now to be someone who liked to be free and on his own, while Bird seemed happiest around other people. What Edna May said next, didn't make Ruddie feel any better.

"The only thing he didn't want to do was to leave you, Ruddie."

CHAPTER 20

THE MAYOR

Edna May and Moss were true to their word and mined out some time with Mayor McLane. The mayor was appalled by Ruddie's ordeal in the Hurst basement and agreed that maybe the story was better left alone, after the police were made aware of who their "John Doe" was.

It was then that Edna May sprang her idea that perhaps Ruddie would be very useful to the Mayor. The boy's recent experiences attested to his resourcefulness and Edna May vouched for his character and willingness to work. As it happened, her timing was good. While Mayor McLane had a cadre of support around him, he had been thinking of adding a "runner" to his staff. His thought was to include someone who he could keep close by, someone who had no previous political connections and someone who was not a threat to any of the diverse groups with whom he was constantly at odds. An enterprising but unknown boy to carry messages and do odd jobs might just work.

In the nine months prior to the fire, McLane's new tenure was constantly under attack. He had won the primary by narrowly defeating the incumbent's entrenched Democratic political machine in a bitter battle. Then, in a highly controversial general election, the thirty-five year old Baltimore blue blood edged the Republican candidate by a mere three hundred ninety-four votes. His opponent refused to concede and the matter was not settled until it went to court. It didn't help the winner's feelings about the party when its leadership refused to foot the bill for the legal battle. In short, the mayor's political enemies were well established and active.

The devastating fire, of course, was another source of conflict for the young mayor. Despite harsh criticism from certain quarters for several decisions made during the blaze, McLane was generally lauded for his leadership and energy in fighting the catastrophe. Afterwards, however, as the mayor struggled to get the charred city back on its feet, he was faced with balancing conflicting opinions on a wide range of topics. Initial praise for his rapid formulation of the Burnt District Committee and the reconstruction plans they set soon devolved into opposition from self-serving politicians, businessmen, contractors, and their attorneys.

The man was under extraordinary stress as he fought to do what he thought best for Baltimore and its future. Yet, he took on the challenge with his usual drive and stamina, seeking creative ways through the morass.

Thinking it through with his friends, in a minor decision, the mayor decided to employ Ruddie. McLane wanted him close at hand both in City Hall and when he was at home on West Preston Street. So, he offered the boy housing in a spare bedroom on the lower floor. Edna May expressed her appreciation, but knowing Ruddie the way that she did, suggested that they find a place close that offered him the freedom she knew he needed. To that end, a room was found in the basement of the Protestant church across the street, thirty yards away. The redhead would ride with his chief each morning to City Hall and return with him in the evening.

Over the next few weeks, Ruddie found himself moving in and out and around the men who ran a major American city. He made no choices and had no responsibilities other than to deliver this note or that file, or to fetch this person or that lunch order, or to count this attendance or note that absence. It would take both age and experience before he would ever understand the mechanics of a complex bicameral government, much less operate effectively within it. But what Ruddie found he could do with some skill was observe people. It wasn't just a matter of recognition; it was more a matter of watching and assessing the interaction among the various powerful people he found himself among. And, he could do it while being virtually invisible.

Ruddie found that after he dropped off a note, a file or a report, if he lingered a bit, melted into the woodwork and observed, he could assess who were his friends and who were his enemies. Not his really, but the mayor's, his boss. This kind of intelligence he kept to himself. It was not part of his job and Mayor McLane never asked him to do it. That changed a few weeks into the work.

The mayor would often labor at home in his upstairs study. He found that it gave him privacy and quiet, away from the constant swarm of those seeking something from him.

Because Ruddie was always to be an arm's length or a shout from the mayor, he would frequently find himself in the kitchen of the house on Preston Street. There, he would drink sweet tea and wait to be summoned. It was inevitable that he would meet and become friends with the McLane maid, Lizzie.

Lizzie Redchurch was a young twenty-two year old who liked talking a lot more than she did cleaning and dusting. In Ruddie, she found a willing listener who seemed to find her opinions of value and her humor quite witty. He also had a crush on the girl that took the form of just sitting and looking at her.

"Ruddie, did you know that Mr. McLane has a sweetheart?"

"A sweetheart?"

"Yeah, you know, someone he's in love with."

"Love?"

"Love. They're going to get married. She's his fiancée."

"Is that so?" Ruddie knew nothing of these things but was hoping Lizzie would tell him.

"Once they marry, she'll come here to live. And I'll go back to being her maid. Ugh!"

"Wait, I thought you worked for the mayor."

"I do, silly. But I really work for Mrs. van Bibber."

"Mrs. …?"

"van Bibber. She brought me with her from Philadelphia."

"So, you …"

"Right. I went to work for her back when her first husband died. He committed suicide, poor man."

"Suicide?" Ruddie hadn't thought about that since the farm.

"That's right. And I can understand that, living with her," said Lizzie being unkind.

"You mean she's hard to live with?" asked the naïve boy.

"That's putting it mildly," she answered. "Let's just say you and I better never call her 'Mary'. She'll be Mrs. van Bibber to us, if you want to keep your job."

"This Mrs. van Bibber, she's mean?"

"As a snake. I've even heard her be sharp with the mayor. I really don't know what he sees in her."

Ruddie, feeling like he was having a real adult conversation, wanted to contribute something. So, after a pause, he said, "I'm not sure the mayor always sees who is friends are."

The boy's timing was unfortunate because behind him Mayor McLane entered the kitchen in time to hear his runner's comment.

"Why would you say that, Ruddie?" asked a clearly offended McLane. "What do you mean, exactly?"

The redhead was mortified. He could say nothing, but just sat there as the color rose on his neck and into his face.

"Lizzie, don't you have something to dust?" the mayor asked the maid.

With a quick "yes sir," the girl disappeared.

"Ruddie, what do you mean I don't know who my friends are?"

Finally, the boy was able to speak. "I'm sorry, Mr. McLane. I meant no harm to you. I would never say anything nasty about you."

"Okay, son, I believe you, but what did you mean?" pressed the mayor.

"Well, sir, sometimes I hear things."

"Yes?"

"Sometimes people forget I'm there and they say things."

"Ruddie, you should know by now that not everyone likes me or wants to help me. "

"Yes, sir, I know that. But sometimes, I hear folks who are supposed to be your friends say things."

"Ruddie, this is very important. Much of my job is pulling people together to get things done. Do you understand that?"

When the boy nodded, the mayor continued. "If I can't trust someone I'm counting on, then I need to know that. Let me give you an example. I need the members of the Burnt District Committee to support the widening of Baltimore Street to prevent fires like the one we've just had. I work to get those votes and I need to know who's with me and who's not. Do you see?"

Ruddie understood. "What can I do to help, sir?"

"I want you to keep doing what you are doing. But I need you to tell me what you hear and who's saying it. It's spying, but it's important spying. Okay?"

"I can do that, Mr. McLane."

With that, over the next three months, Ruddie became not just a runner for the mayor but also his eyes and ears. In the following weeks, the boy became a valuable asset in the mayor's arsenal in getting the Commission's plans executed.

In the process, the boy's own eyes were opened to how difficult his employer's task was. It wasn't overenthusiasm that awakened Ruddie to the number of real enemies Robert M. McLane had. They were out there and they were busy.

There were obvious opponents like Clay Timanus, the president of the Second Branch of the City Council, and Frank Wachter, the defeated Republication mayoral candidate and several businessmen whose buildings were dynamited at McLane's direction during the fire. But there were civilian members of the mayor's own Commission, east coast contractors who lost huge reconstruction bids, members of organized crime and democratic supporters angry at the mayor's appointing independents into key jobs.

Most of the time, Ruddie was unaware of the various connections and reasons for the enmity, but he could remember a name and face. And these observations he loyally reported to his boss. This information became invaluable to the mayor who made use of it to negotiate his way past the shoals around an issue. For Ruddie, this duty became a way to get to know the mayor in a way he may never have had otherwise. As result, the redhead started to become closer to the city's leader than he had with any other adult in his short life, aside from his mother of course.

There was one exception to his loyalty. That exception was Mary van Bibber. Ruddie had been introduced to the mayor's fiancée at the house on Preston Street. It had not gone well and the boy was left feeling decidedly commonplace. Lizzie had been caustic about the woman, but she had been right. As cold as Mrs. van Bibber was to him, what disturbed him the most about her was her demands of the mayor that showed a distinct lack of recognition for the burdens her husband-to-be was carrying.

When Ruddie spotted her in a carriage with another gentleman and on another occasion coming out of a restaurant with the same gentleman, he had said nothing to the mayor. He might have described the two as acting romantically toward each other, but his inexperience in such matters made him question whether that was the case. As a result, the boy said nothing. Later, while waiting in the Preston Street kitchen, he observed the same gentleman being introduced as Mrs. van Bibber's brother-in-law, Claude, who had remained close to her after his brother's death. This was enough for the boy to remain silent.

CHAPTER 21

BITTER GRAPES

In the middle of May, Robert M. McLane married the Philadelphia socialite, Mary van Bibber. The wedding was held in Washington, DC in almost the fashion of an elopement. Mayor McLane wished to avoid ostentation, as he was wont to do, and Mary wished to avoid her new husband's parents who opposed the wedding. So, after a small ceremony, the McLane's returned to Baltimore and Mrs. McLane took over the household on Preston Street.

The relationship between Ruddie and Robert McLane continued to grow as the mayor learned that he really could trust his young operative. The mayor's distractions increased with married life but he continued to be kind to Ruddie, treating him with respect. As a result, the boy was energized with a sense of purpose and reveled in the freedom of movement the job allowed. Ruddie, perhaps for the first time in his life, was content.

While Mrs. McLane ignored him completely, she didn't interfere in his duties for the mayor. The only change brought on by the marriage that he could see was that Mrs. McLane closely managed Lizzie to the degree that there were no more idle conversations with the girl in the kitchen.

The morning of May 30 was a lazy one for Ruddie. It was Decoration Day; all city offices were closed and the mayor had planned to enjoy the holiday with his wife. So, the boy slept until ten, then finally stirred himself to go find breakfast at a nearby café. As he walked down the block, he noticed the mayor across the street chatting amiably with a gentleman. He waved to Ruddie then parted from the conversation and continued to stroll the block. When Ruddie returned to his room in the church basement, he spied the mayor again laughing and joking with yet another man he had met on the street.

It was the boy's plan to walk to the Maryland Theater on Liberty Street to see what they were calling a "movie." The show was called *The Great Train Robbery* and Ruddie couldn't wait to see it.

When he returned around three thirty in the afternoon, he noticed a crowd gathered on Preston Street. As he realized the swarm hovered in front of number twenty-nine, he began to run. There were neighborhood people certainly, but also cops. He skidded to a halt and in the process ran into a man carrying a black bag. The man was rushing as well and Ruddie heard someone say, "The doctor is here, at last!"

Squeezing past him, coming out of the front door was Lizzie. She was crying and began to run down the block. Ruddie caught up to her and stopped her.

In tears, she sobbed. "Ruddie, not now. Mrs. McLane has sent me to fetch her friend!"

"Lizzie, what's happened? Tell me!"

The girl shook her head and finally got out, "Mr. McLane has shot himself!"

"What did you say …?" But Lizzie was gone in a sprint.

Ruddie turned back to the door and attempted to bolt up the stairs, but it was no use. There were too many people jammed in the doorway. When a second doctor arrived, the boy was pushed out into the street, where he stood among the shocked gawkers.

"I can't imagine why the mayor would want to kill himself," said one.

"How do you know it was suicide?" asked another.

"I was just talking to him this morning. He seemed fine. It must have been an accident," said a man who could have been the one Ruddie had seen with the mayor earlier.

"I just saw him having lunch with that new wife of his," commented someone else.

More police arrived and a battery of official looking men also showed up, but the only news Ruddie was getting was the opinions of the onlookers. He realized that he was not getting into the house, so he walked across the street and sat on the church steps and put his head in his hands. Then he did something he had not done since his mother died. He prayed to God, any god that would listen. He prayed that the man Ruddie had begun to love was not dead.

Eventually, around five o'clock, word came out of the house that Robert M. McLane was dead. It was suicide, they said, but that made no sense to Ruddie. Wouldn't he have sensed it, if the mayor was so far gone that he felt he had to take his own life? The boy felt like he had a knack for reading people so this was more than shocking, it was impossible. So, he sat there on the steps into the evening, stunned.

Within Ruddie's confusion, he began a process of emotional self-preservation. Once again, he had gotten close to someone, only to lose them. It was the story of his life, first his mother and Nora, then the Twiggs, then Bird, and now Mr. McLane. How many times did it take before he learned his lesson? Well, he had learned it now.

Some believe that children have an amazing ability to adapt to even radical change. While that may be true, others believe that kids exposed to a traumatic event have difficulty dealing with the emotions the event precipitates. Under those circumstances, it is said that the young will act out as a substitute for managing their feelings.

Ruddie went to his room, packed his duffle and fished out the money he had stashed in his mattress. It wasn't a lot but it was what he managed to save over the last three months working for the mayor. In the process, he began to think about Edna May. No one was kinder to him than she was. Would she leave him as well? He wasn't going to give her that chance. He would go to see her for the last time.

Ruddie walked to The Belvedere only to be told at the front desk that Edna May was not there. While they weren't sure where she was, they were happy to give her a message from him. Ruddie felt some urgency to talk to her, at the very least to let her know about Mayor McLane. It was a guess on the boy's part that she was at The Auditorium because that's where she normally was when she wasn't in the hotel. It would not be unusual for her to be doing a show on the holiday evening. So, he asked for directions and got them, but missed a comment from the desk clerk as he hurried away.

The Auditorium and all of Baltimore's Theater District on North Howard Street had been spared the fire's rage. It was located only about five or six blocks away and Ruddie felt he could negotiate the dark streets quickly and safely alone. He was wrong about that though; he hadn't gotten far when he was attacked. Out of an alley a dark figure flew at him, trying to tackle his legs. This spooked the boy, but then he recognized his assailant by the light of a street lamp. General Sherman was as frantic as ever, but maybe a little dirtier than he was when he had bolted away from Bird and him nearly six months earlier.

"Now where have you been?" Ruddie asked the dog, as he bent and scratched the animal behind his wire-stiff ears.

The pooch was ecstatic, as if he had been looking for Ruddie all this time and finally found him. Ruddie felt this and smiled, but only briefly. He stood and stepped away from the dog.

"You left me. And you stink. You smell like smoke. Go on, git!" The boy pushed the animal away with his foot.

This didn't deter General Sherman in the least. He continued to circle the boy and bounce as if he had springs on his paws. Ruddie ignored the little beast and walked away at a rapid pace. Regardless, General Sherman was on his heels and he wasn't about to lose the boy again.

As Ruddie drew near to his destination, he could see the lights of the vibrant area, but when he arrived at the address given to him, he got yet another surprise. The lights were coming from another theater's marquee. Next door, where The Auditorium was supposed to be, was a vacant lot piled with brick rubble, twisted steel girders, and other debris of a structure that had been torn down. It looked exactly like the hundreds of buildings ruined by the fire and demolished by the work crews attempting to clean up the disaster.

Running his hands through his red mop, Ruddie looked around him. The street, though well lit, was quieter than it would be when the numerous theaters let out after their shows. He was at a loss as to what to do. He had no idea where he might find Edna May now. He pushed General Sherman away for the tenth time and glared at him. That's when he noticed the sign over the door of a tavern across the street—The Diamond. Wasn't that the name of the place Edna May had taken Bird for lunch?

As a last resort, Ruddie crossed the street and peeked in the window. The place was closed on a Monday night, despite the holiday, but there was a light on inside.

CHAPTER 22

IN THE DIAMOND

Ruddie pushed on the brass plate next to the stained glass panel in the front door of the Diamond Cafe, found it open and walked in. General Sherman flashed in behind him as the door was closing. When the redhead took the two steps down into the main taproom, a man yelled at him.

"The place is closed. Come back tomorrow!" Then he said, "Hey! You can't bring that dog in here. Get out!"

The less than warm greeting came from one of two men sitting at the bar sharing a pitcher of beer. One was counting receipts, the other reading a newspaper.

The reader looked up and smiled. It was Moss Tilghman, Edna May's friend and the man who helped Ruddie get the job with Mayor McLane.

"Hold on, Frank. I know this young man. This is the heroic Ruddie Quick come to visit us."

"Moss, I don't care who the kid is he can't bring that mangy mutt in here, or we'll have Sanitation down on us again."

Ignoring his companion, Moss said, "And if I'm not mistaken, that's his dog, the equally heroic General Sherman!"

Before anything else could be said, Ruddie stopped and looked down at the dog. "He's not my dog."

"Then, I'm going to get rid of him." Moss' friend stood and stepped toward the animal, but stopped when General Sherman emitted a low growl.

"Wait, Frank," said Moss. "Let's see why Ruddie has come. I suspect he needs our help." Then he rose and walked over to Ruddie and said, "We just heard about the mayor. Very sad. Are you all right?"

Ruddie said nothing but began to tear up. He turned quickly to go. At that, Moss put his arm around the boy, took his duffle and guided him to one of the tables in the café.

"Ruddie, what can I do? Please let me help."

The redhead felt lost and alone and embarrassed by his tears. But Moss' gentle manner and Ruddie's desperation combined to allow himself to be folded into the big man's arms. The crying started in earnest then.

After a bit, Ruddie calmed down but found speech difficult. Moss sat with him and coaxed him back, trying to communicate that he was among friends without asking anything from the miserable boy.

Finally, Moss said, "I bet you could stand something to eat. I bet the General could as well by the look of him. Frank, I'll stay here with Ruddie. Can you see if you can find a little something in the kitchen? I think some of that turkey's back there."

"Frank" was Frank Van Sant, Moss' close friend and the managing partner of The Diamond. He nodded, left, and soon emerged with a glass of milk and the fixings for a turkey sandwich. For the General, to make amends and to avoid getting bitten, Frank found the scraps from the steaks Moss had trimmed in preparation for the next night's patrons. That seemed to put the manager in solid with the dog.

Between bites of the sandwich, Ruddie explained that he had come looking for Edna May to tell her about Mayor McLane, but didn't realize that the theater had been torn down. Once he got started talking, the redhead's day poured out of him, ending with the disbelief that his employer committed suicide.

"I really liked him. I can't believe he shot himself. I would have known. He was good to me and I think I helped him. I guess not enough. I thought we could work together for a long time. I should never have expected that."

When it looked like the boy had no more to say, Moss offered, "Ruddie, whether Robert did or did not take his own life makes little difference to me, personally. I knew the mayor as a real leader, someone I respected. What he has managed to accomplish for this city in the last three months may never be fully appreciated. You were a part of that, and you should be proud of it."

"It's over now isn't it though? And I'm out of a job. It doesn't pay to get too involved with anyone."

Moss could sense easily enough that the boy's sadness wasn't about the loss of a job. He knew Ruddie's background from Edna May and he began to see why he was so distraught. It went beyond the death of the mayor. As independent as Ruddie was, his whole life had been a story of loss. Maybe that's why he prized his independence so much.

"Ruddie, it's hard, and sometimes we get disappointed but I think we humans need other people. Not all the time, maybe, but if we're by ourselves too much, then we're unhappy too. Everyone has to find their own balance between being by themselves and being with those we like or even love."

Ruddie listened to the older man and understood most of it, but seemed unconvinced. Moss didn't press the issue any further. Instead, he asked his visitor if he had a place to stay the night. Ruddie explained that he still had the room below the Protestant church but he really didn't want to go back there. The two men had already planned to stay over in the café that night, as they often did, so they made arrangements for the boy in one of the upstairs rooms. Frank said that he would lock up, then try to clean General Sherman up a little before he brought him up to Ruddie. At that, the redhead reminded the man that the dog was not his.

CHAPTER 23

ONE TIME FRIENDS

At about the time Ruddie was getting the news that Mayor McLane was dead, Edna May was back at The Boys Home talking to Adolf Franz about an idea she had that would see the placement of more of the director's orphans. Word was spreading rapidly around the city that the mayor had been shot and the news reached The Boys Home quicker than most places. This broke up Edna May's meeting because one of her first thoughts was for Ruddie.

As it happened, while the boy was seeking Edna May at the Belvedere, she was looking for him at the Protestant church. When she finally returned to the hotel, the desk clerk spotted her coming in and let her know that the redheaded boy had been looking for her. While Ruddie didn't leave a message, the hotel man mentioned that he had asked for directions to The Auditorium.

Edna May realized that Ruddie was looking for her most likely because he was upset. She turned on her heels, hailed a carriage in front of the hotel and directed the driver to get to Howard Street as quickly as possible.

When the former actress arrived, the crowd was letting out of the Academy of Music, but it dispersed rapidly and soon Edna May was one of the few remaining on Howard Street. Ruddie was nowhere to be found. She looked over at The Diamond but, as she did, she saw the lights go out. So, she returned to The Belvedere hoping Ruddie would retrace his steps.

Back in her suite, Edna May began to pace the living room. Then she began to straighten cushions and wipe non-existent dust from tables in an effort to keep busy. In the process, she noticed that the day's mail had been delivered and that one envelop contained Bird's clumsy scrawl. She opened it and read. He had started to write to her regularly to let her know how he was doing, and she thought that sweet, but each letter ended the same way—with a question about Ruddie. This letter was no different.

Edna May fretted over her one-time, redheaded charge. In fact, while she knew Ruddie needed his freedom, she still felt responsible for him. He was now probably thirteen years old, but in a lot of ways he was still a boy. And he still needed to be loved. And she did.

CHAPTER 24

AESOP'S FOX

When Ruddie woke the next morning, it took him a minute to get oriented in his strange surroundings. He had slept soundly, despite General Sherman's persistence in lying on the boy's feet at the bottom of the bed. The dog was nowhere to be found at the moment, however.

Hearing indistinct voices downstairs, the redhead rose and made his way down to them. He paused on the stairs next to an autographed photograph of a jockey and listened.

"I'm sure he was under a lot of stress, but it's hard to imagine that he took his own life, Moss. The man was just married two weeks ago."

"Frank, we don't know what happened. All we have is what's in *The Sun*." There was the sound of a rustling newspaper.

"But if it was an accident, it seems odd that there were powder burns on the side of his head."

"Ah. I see we're back to playing Sherlock Holmes again."

"I'm not saying it was murder, but there are a lot of questions here."

"I worked with Robert on the Citizen's Emergency Committee after the fire. The man had a lot of enemies and that's the truth," responded Moss.

"Yeah, and isn't it ironic that his biggest pain-in-the-ass, that City Council guy, Timanus, now inherits the job and all of McLane's problems."

"Frank, Clay Timanus is a good man too. Just has different ideas about rebuilding downtown. It's likely that he'll be the beneficiary of a construction boom that Robert started."

"And what about his wife?"

"What about her?"

"I never did trust anyone from Philadelphia."

"Is that intuition I hear? What happened to reason, Sherlock?"

With that, Ruddie walked into the taproom. The men were sitting at one of the barroom's tables reading the news and drinking coffee. General Sherman was under the table chewing on a bone. When the dog spotted the boy, he picked up the bone and trotted over to him, but Ruddie ignored the animal.

"Morning, Ruddie," said Moss. "How'd you sleep? Want some breakfast?" He folded the newspaper and threw it up onto the bar.

"I'm not hungry," answered the boy.

"Sure you are," said Frank, rising. "How about some eggs and bacon and a couple of Moss' biscuits? There's orange juice too."

"I'll get it, Frank," said Moss also rising. "Want more coffee?"

Frank nodded, but Ruddie said nothing. Moss went into the kitchen anyway.

Trying to make conversation, Frank asked, "Ruddie, how do you like The Diamond? It's owned by one of the Orioles." He pointed around the room to all of the various sports memorabilia hanging on the walls.

"Okay, I guess."

Sports had never been a big part of Ruddie's life, in fact, they had been non-existent. Bird had told him about baseball and talked about the Orioles, but he had no clear idea of how the sport was played or who played it.

His response killed Frank's line of chit chat, leaving the manager no idea of what to say to his morose guest. He wasn't going to bring up what everyone in Baltimore was talking about that morning, so they sat awkwardly in silence until Moss emerged with breakfast.

Ruddie picked at the bacon on the plate at first, decided maybe he was hungry and began to eat in earnest.

"Moss, I've got to get ready to open up. Let me know what supplies you need for the kitchen this week when you get a chance. I'll be around."

Then the manager turned back and said to Ruddie, "Oh, by the way, you left your duffle bag down here last night. I put a few things in there in case you get hungry." With that, Moss and Ruddie were left alone at the table with General Sherman settling back down underneath, after he made sure Frank wasn't going to produce any more bones.

"Ruddie, does Edna May know where you are?" asked the cook.

"She's not my mother," the boy said petulantly.

When Moss looked at him, Ruddie seemed to regret his sharp words and said, "No, I guess she doesn't. That's why I came here looking for her."

"Would you like me to let her know?"

"Okay. But I'm not going back to the hotel. Just tell her thanks for every-thing."

"Nothing else?"

"No."

Moss, recalling very well the conversation with the boy the previous night, nodded. Then he asked, "What are you planning to do? Where are you going to go?"

"I don't know. Away. Maybe I can get a job with the railroad."

"The railroad, huh? That's a tough business. You may be a little young for that yet."

"You're not the first person to tell me that," replied the boy, a little of his ill-humor returning.

Moss was patient and said, "You know, you still have time to decide what you want to do. Whatever you do next doesn't have to be forever. Sometimes it takes a while to figure it out. I tried a lot of things before I realized I loved cooking."

"Cooking?"

"Yeah, that's what I do and I never get tired of it. Maybe that's why I love it. Or, maybe I never get tired of it because I love it." Moss gave Ruddie a small grin.

The world's many opportunities were not something Ruddie thought much about, of course, but the idea of cooking food was so foreign to him that maybe Moss' comment opened the door of possibilities a crack.

"Let me ask you what I asked your friend, Bird. What is it you like to do?"

Ruddie remembered what Bird had said when Moss asked him. And al-though he and Bird were different, there was at least one thing they had in common. So, he said, "I like being on the water."

"Is that so? Me too. I've spent a fair amount of time on the water myself," replied Moss. "What I remember most about it was the feeling of freedom it gives you. Especially when you sail by yourself. Then, it's just you and your thoughts out there. When I learned to sail, I found peace."

At that, Ruddie looked up. This was new, but it resonated loudly with him.

"In fact, the folks Bird is staying with tell me that he's been out on the water."

"He has?"

"You might like it. Ever think about trying sailing?"

Such a thing had never even crossed the boy's mind, but the idea was stirring for the very reasons Moss said he liked it. However, Ruddie had started to get the feeling that he was being manipulated in the conversation. He sensed that Moss, as well intentioned as he may be, was nudging him in a particular direction. He was convinced of it with the man's next comment.

"I know my friends would be happy to have you visit. I could write them for you and maybe you could see Bird. In fact, I know a captain who's sailing to Crisfield this week. He's got a schooner called the *James A. Whiting* in The Basin now. He could take you."

Now Ruddie once again was on full alert. Not only was the man suggesting what he should do, he was trying to settle him with new people. This was not going to happen.

"Moss, all of that sounds fine and I appreciate your offer, but I don't think so. I want to be on my own for a while."

"Ruddie ..."

The boy stood, waggled a "no thanks" with his hand and said, "I think I'll be going now. Thanks for the breakfast. And thanks for your advice, and putting me up last night."

"Ruddie, let me—"

"No, really, I'll be okay. I just need to get going."

With that, Ruddie picked up his duffle, shook Moss' hand and hurried out the front entry without looking back. General Sherman was on his heels and managed to get out as the door closed.

Ruddie walked south on Howard Street toward his old newspaper territory. He really didn't know what he was going to do and was lost in a kaleidoscopic reverie of the people he was leaving behind—the mayor, Edna May, Bird, Moss. They all had been kind to him and they now were all gone. He wasn't feeling lonely especially, maybe a little sorry for himself though. He was alone. And that's the way he wanted it. Wasn't it? Yes, because his experience told him that it was too painful otherwise.

With no real plan, he thought that maybe he would go look at what was left of the Hurst Building. He turned left on German street and entered The Burnt District. All of the National Guardsmen who patrolled the area and kept the looters at bay during the last three months were gone now. There were police patrols on horseback of course but many fewer than there were in the early days. Aside from businessmen touring the past in order to plan for the future, the only groups in evidence were the crews of street sweepers, the "White Wings," so named for the white overalls they wore. The sound of their shovels scraping concrete filled the air as they loaded drays to be dumped on barges destined for various sites around the Chesapeake. Even the number of curious visitors had fallen off, since the city had demolished most of the ghost-like husks of burned-out buildings.

So, he was by himself as he stood and looked at nothing but a dune of bricks and a mound of twisted steel and concrete. It was hard to imagine now the tall buildings that used to line the narrow streets, blocking out the sun and creating narrow wind tunnels that drove the flames that awful Sunday morning.

Ruddie imagined the shade of Big Russ entombed under the rubble. He saw again the onlookers watching the blaze with him, their upturned faces reflecting its light and heat. He recalled their terror when the horrific blast blew the roof off the building and sent flaming debris in all directions. He smelled the smoke and heard once more the panicked shouts of firemen directing ineffective gushes of water from the tangle of hoses snaking their way down the street. It was time to go and never come back.

The redhead walked away from the destruction with the vague idea that he would head toward the B&O's Camden Rail Station four or five blocks away. Maybe he would travel south. General Sherman trotted along with him despite the fact that Ruddie didn't even acknowledge his existence. The dog seemed content with the boy's company and asked nothing of his companion.

When he reached the station, Ruddie stopped walking, halted by his lack of real direction. He didn't go in but found a bench outside that allowed a distant view of the busy harbor basin down Conway Street. He sat next to his bag and stared straight ahead, not actually looking at anything. General Sherman hopped up on the seat next to the redhead and put his head on his paws.

Ruddie finally looked down at the dog when the pooch started to nose the duffle bag. Evidently, he'd caught wind of whatever Moss' friend put in there.

"Oh, now I see why you've been following me. Okay, but just because I feed you, doesn't mean we're friends."

Ruddie opened the bag to investigate and found a baloney sandwich, an apple and a few oatmeal cookies. He gave half of the sandwich to the dog, then noticed an envelope that had not been there before. Inside was fifty dollars in cash and a note. The note read: "Ruddie, good luck and all the best. Come see us if you ever need some friends. Moss and Frank."

The redhead showed no reaction to the kindness and resumed looking off into the distance. He thought about all that happened to him in the last year and all of the things he had done. He thought about all of the people he'd met and all of those who were now gone. Then he thought of his mother and the strengths she had given him.

Before long, he looked down at General Sherman who was staring back expecting the other half of his lunch. Ruddie heaved a huge sigh, reached over and scratched the mutt behind the ears and said:

"Well, General, how would you like to go see Bird again?"

The End

Appendix I

Author's Notes

Aesop's Fox is a work of fiction and is not in any way an attempt to establish a historical record. Just the same, I have tried to capture the life on the C&O Canal and in the city of Baltimore accurately for the years 1903-1904. The primary characters in the novel are products of my imagination; however, many others appearing or referenced in these pages are not fictional and I have attempted to capture them as reflected in the generally accepted historical record.

Aesop's parable of *The Fox and the Grapes* is a well-loved fable and is perhaps the best known of his twenty tales involving the fox as the cunning trickster or the resourceful solver of problems. Close reading of the novel may find several of the fox's tales in the travels of Ruddie, but its focus is clearly (I hope) on the story of the grapes. More specifically, it tries to reflect the natural human tendency to devalue those things we cannot have or achieve. Those that study or write of this refer to it as "cognitive dissonance" or the propensity to use disdain to reduce the conflict between desire and its frustration. Ruddie is certainly frustrated in his relationships even though he seeks new ones one after the other, to the point that eventually he mistrusts and rejects them. It was my faltering attempt to turn the fox's disdainful departure on its head by providing Ruddie with the strength of character to give the leap at the grapes one more try.

The history underlying the building and operation of the Chesapeake and Ohio Canal from George Washington's original idea and the start of its construction in 1828 to its eventual demise in 1924 is long and fascinating. Its function as the engine that pushed the country off the Atlantic Coast, through the Appalachians and into the Midwest and beyond is undeniable. And the story of its relationship with its parallel economic generators, the Potomac River and the B&O Railroad, is a story of American muscle and ingenuity. However, the C&O Canal is not just an economic story. It is every bit the story of the individuals who built and plied the canal or otherwise kept it operating all of those years. I have listed several worthwhile reads in Appendix II that not only do a fine job of describing almost every inch of the waterway, but also tell the stories of those who lived it.

I have always had a passing fascination with the stories behind why owners name their boats the way they do. Whether it's a Chesapeake Bay runabout named *"Hers II"* or it's *Minnie B. Welcome*, I find they say much more about the owner than the craft. The Twigg's canal barge is fictious, as is its name, but I chose it for its sound and typicality of the boats that plied the canal prior to the days of the B&O Railroad's dominance.

Readers might spot two different spellings of Allegany in the text. The reason is that they refer to two different counties, Allegany County in Maryland and Allegheny County in Pennsylvania, the home of the Allegheny Coal Company.

The history of the relationship between the C&O Canal and the B&O Railroad is a long and complicated one, as is the ownership of those two economic catalysts. Specific details and timing may be found in the sources listed in Appendix II below.

The National Parks Service web sites (https://www.nps.gov) and a number of other sources listed in Appendix II provide a wealth of information on the C&O Canal and include details on the remarkable engineering feat that was the waterway, including the Paw Paw Tunnel, the mechanics of its seventy-four locks, its towpaths and many other aspects of the canal.

The NPS sites also provide fascinating reading in regards to the human stories and myths that have roots along the canal, including the very real tragedy of the Spong Family (www.nps.gov/choh/learn/historyculture/thespongchild ren.htm).

After the Civil War, when the country was being rebuilt and expanding exponentially into the world's greatest industrial power, it was a particular American mania to build a railroad. Lines and spurs were being built not just between major cities, but also between towns and minor cities all across the country. While consolidation and monopoly became the game later in the century, railroads, like the Western Maryland Railway (WM), laid track and ran coal, people, mail and many other things very successfully for many years in the shadow of the B&Os, the Pennsylvania Railroads and other giants of the industry. The WM's main line ran between Hagerstown and Baltimore, with construction beginning in 1857 and completing the run through partnership and consolidation in 1873. Three years later, the WM completed a connection from Hagerstown to Williamsport, in order to access coal traffic from the Chesapeake and Ohio Canal. By the time

Ruddie and Bird rode the WM in 1903, the company had connected its lines to B&O lines and built an extension further west to Cumberland.

Ruddie and Bird's eight mile ride from Williamsport to Hagerstown was on the top of what was known as The Blue Ridge Trolley. The trolley was a part of a larger electric railway system owned and operated by the Hagerstown & Frederick Railway. The system was begun in 1896 and connected most of Western Maryland's towns and cities for over fifty years. The Hagerstown & Frederick had always run what originally amounted to a side business, selling electricity to customers in the vicinity of its operations. Although the railway declined, the electric utility branch prospered and grew into the dominant electric company in a four-state area—the Potomac Edison Co.

I enjoyed putting together the scene of Ruddie and Bird stopping in The Mount Vernon Coffee House (fictious) when they first arrived in Baltimore. The description of the café's front window comes directly from a 1930 prize winning photograph (The Coffee House) taken by the great *Baltimore Sun* photographer and chronicler of the city and state, A. Aubrey Bodine. Bodine's work (1927-1970) is endlessly fascinating and has earned him numerous awards and an international reputation. Admittedly, I used the 1930 prices on the window as a stand-in for 1903 prices. I felt this reasonable because these food costs during the Great Depression seemed to compare favorably to 1903 prices as found in the Morris County Library in Whippany, New Jersey (e.g., Sirloin steak .20/lb. and "Fancy Rose" potatoes .59/half bushel).

The monument that the boys discover is of course that which was dedicated in 1829 to honor George Washington. It is the work of American architect Robert Mills and is the country's first major monument dedicated to the father of our country. The 178 foot, eight inch Doric column is the centerpiece of the Mount Vernon urban square in the Mount Vernon-Belvedere neighborhood. It holds a ground floor gallery, offering digital exhibits on its construction, the history of the area and the life and accomplishments of the General and President. Energetic visitors may climb its 227 steps to enjoy a view of the surrounding area.

Since the middle of the nineteenth century, the Mount Vernon area has been the center of Baltimore art and culture, not to mention its highest levels of wealth and society. The buildings surrounding the square's four parks, noted by Ruddie and Bird, include The Peabody Institute, The Walters Art Museum, Enoch Pratt's Central Library, The Maryland Center for History and Culture (formerly, the Maryland Historical Society), the Baltimore Cathedral (The Basilica of the

National Shrine of the Assumption off the Blessed Virgin Mary), the Baltimore School for the Arts and a number of impressive mansions, including those of the Pratt and the Garrett families.

The nanny's joke regarding the Father of Our Country is intended for Baltimore insiders and I hope that others will forgive me an easter egg I just couldn't resist.

As I was researching a place for the boys to land in Baltimore, with the help of The Maryland Center for History and Culture, I found a 1903 map of the city. This document showed a building marked as "Boys' Home" at the northwest corner of Calvert and Pleasant Streets. Further digging in the archives of the *Baltimore Sun* produced a finely detailed article about the place from 1956 by John L. Schimf who had actually been one of the boys living there at the turn of the century. This happy circumstance got even better when I noticed on the same map that across the street on the northeast corner of that intersection was a Jesuit catholic church, specifically Saint Francis Xavier Catholic Church for Colored People, built in 1836. It seems that, at times, the church also operated a small school. With the stars in alignment, I had what I needed to get my two fugitives settled, albeit segregated and directly across the street from each other.

Edna May Drambauer was first introduced in my novel, *No Slave To Reason*. She is a fictional character drawn from the very real, comedic actress, Edna May, found in The Maryland Center for History and Culture's collection of 1897 playbills and other ephemera for The Auditorium Theater. Edna May's background, her personality, career, her relationship with James Lawrence Kernan and her rise to stardom are all figments of my imagination. However, her popularity can be easily and plausibly surmised from the number of times she appeared in the archive.

The Howard Street Theater District was as vibrant in 1903 as it was in the 1890s. (See my second novel in the Baltimore Series, *No Slave To Reason*, for greater detail on this area of the city, its theaters and The Diamond Cafe.) I've taken some liberty in *Aesop's Fox* with the history of The Auditorium at 516 North Howard Street for purposes of the plot. The theater was actually torn down in April of 1903, not in 1904, and rebuilt by September of 1904 as a venue for vaudeville and "moving pictures." More recent history of the Auditorium saw the building rebranded as The Mayfair Theater in 1941.

To clarify the history of Baltimore's major broadsheet newspapers mentioned in the novel, *The Baltimore Sun* began publishing in 1837 and now is the only remaining daily newspaper in the city. Its evening edition, *The Evening Sun*, began in 1910 and was published until 1992. *The Sun* began operations in 1851 out of its "Iron Building" at South and East Baltimore Streets, so called for its revolutionary cast iron front design reflecting the earliest "skyscraper" construction technique. The building was destroyed in its entirety by the 1904 fire.

The *Baltimore News-American* was formed by a final merger of two papers, the *Baltimore News-Post* and *The Baltimore Sunday American*, in 1964. Those newspapers each had a long history before the merger, in particular the *Baltimore American* which could trace its lineage unbroken to at least 1796. *The Baltimore News American* closed its doors in May of 1986.

The *Baltimore Morning Herald* (1900-1904) building stood at the northwest corner of St. Paul and East Fayette Streets, on the northern edge of the "Burnt District" and was completely destroyed by the fire. The novel mentions H. L. Mencken, the "Bard of Baltimore," as a reporter for *The Herald*. Mencken was, in fact, both reporter and editor of the paper. Readers can follow the fire and the author's impressions of it as he moved around the city in his work *Newspaper Days*. (1941), the second volume of his autobiographical trilogy.

The Hotel Belvedere, opened in December of 1903, was an irresistible venue for me as the plot of the novel developed. Its beauty and history would be sufficient for a story all its own. Some of the most famous and influential people in the world passed through its grand entrance. A 2003 *Baltimore Magazine* article listed its patrons as "...Royalty and presidents. Movie stars and music idols. Sports heroes and global explorers. Gangsters and detectives. Novelists and newspapermen. Developers and financiers." In short, anyone who was anyone in 1903 responded to the catch phrase "Meet me at the Belvedere." A *Newsweek* article rediscovered the hotel recently (September, 2020) and focused on its more infamous history, mentioning its many ghosts, its history of murder, numerous scandals and naked women roaming the halls. Where better to put Edna May up?

I cannot attempt to do the Great Baltimore Fire justice in my novel and seek only to give readers an inkling of what it was like. Interested readers have a world of excellent research from which to draw (See Appendix II below), including edge-of-your-seat written detail and mind-blowing photographs that capture the devastation during the fire and its aftermath. Having said that, I'd especially like to mention the work of Peter B. Petersen and his wonderful book,

The Great Baltimore Fire, published in 2004 by The Maryland Historical Society. His writing puts you there, minute by minute, hour by hour and the hundreds of photographs he has gathered create an indelible image of a time and place never to be forgotten.

Perhaps to state the obvious, I have taken the fiction writer's liberty of inventing the way the fire started. While no one really knows how it began, the most commonly cited explanation is that a lit cigar was dropped through a grate in the sidewalk outside of the Hurst Building. Somehow the butt made it from there into the basement that was filled with dry goods, as described in the novel.

The hungry Ruddie made his way to The Lexington Market to pilfer his meals. The market is the oldest market in America, having been in existence since 1782. Built originally on land that was a part of the John Eager Howard estate, by the middle of the nineteenth century it was considered "the largest, most famous market on earth" (https://lexingtonmarket.com/history). The Lexington Market was the largest in a network of public markets that supplied the city's neighborhoods beginning in 1771. By 1904, Baltimore was served by eight other public markets, including the Broadway Market (1786), the Centre Market (1787), the Hollins Market (1838), the Cross Street Market (1846), the Richmond Market (1853), the Avenue Market (1871), the Belair Market (1871) and the Northeast Market (1885).

Faidley's Seafood is a family-owned business that has been operating in the Lexington Market since John and Flossie Faidley started the business in 1886. The market stall is probably the best known seafood icon in a city that lives on what has come out of the Chesapeake since the days of Cecil Calvert.

The town of Crisfield on Maryland's Eastern Shore and the fictional Swann family who live there played a significant role in my novel, *No Slave To Reason*. To fully understand why Moss felt the town and the family the perfect place for Bird to alight, readers may want to visit the novel and its Author's Notes.

The death of Mayor Robert McLane in December of 1904 remains one of Baltimore's enduring mysteries. Over the years both professional and amateur sleuths have attempted to discover that one clue that would answer the question: Was it really suicide as reported in 1904 by the authorities, an accident, murder or something else? Fortunately or unfortunately, the story has a raft of interesting contradictions, including his reported untroubled attitude just prior to his death, the recency of his marriage, his wife's history, the many enemies the mayor had made politically and otherwise, the money and plans involved in rebuilding the city and more. The one common denominator in the entire episode is that Mayor McLane's death came as huge a shock to the city just as it did to Ruddie Quick.

Despite the fact that conspiracy theorists enjoy pointing the finger at the mayor's new bride, Mary van Bibber, there seems to be no hard evidence as to her involvement in the death. Any speculation along this line seems to derive from a series of circumstantial occurrences and a fondness for the lurid. I have taken the liberty, probably unfairly, of providing Mrs. van Bibber with a less than endearing personality. This is simply intended to muddy the waters around the death for the reader without actually offering a solution to the mayor's demise. I offer my apologies to anyone who this may offend.

For years, chroniclers of the fire maintained that there were no deaths incurred that were directly related to the fire. Mr. Peterson's book, however, while calling them unconfirmed, mentions three firefighters who died as a result of pneumonia and a fourth who succumbed to tuberculosis. The scholar also notes that he came across a Johns Hopkins undergraduate who discovered a death certificate and a small newspaper article from the 1904 *Baltimore Sun* that described the death of an African-American man on Bowley's Wharf during the fire. True or not, that's all I needed to create tension in Ruddie (fearing Bird's death) and anger in Moss (capturing the cultural mindset of 1904).

The Diamond Café (sometimes listed as Tavern) was located at 519 North Howard Street in the middle of Baltimore's Theater District and directly across the street from The Auditorium. The Diamond was begun by two members of the championship Baltimore Orioles of the 1890s, Hall of Famers John McGraw and Wilbert Robinson. The café plays a prominent role in the first two novels of my Baltimore Trilogy and makes a cameo appearance here as it makes its exit from the stage. Note that by 1904, McGraw had moved on to New York and sold his interest to "Uncle Robbie" who continued to operate the tavern until well after his playing days.

JTE
August 2020

APPENDIX II

CONTRIBUTORS, SOURCES, AND SUGGESTED READING

Books

Aesop. *Aesopica (Aesop's Fables)*.

Aesop. *The Classic Treasury of Aesop's Fables*. New York: Running Press, 1999.

Baltimore Sun Media Group. *Baltimore Memories: A Pictorial History of the 1800s Through the 1930s*. Baltimore: Pediment Publishing, 2017.

Bodine, Jennifer B. *Bodine's City: The Photography of A. Aubrey Bodine*. Atglen, PA: Shiffer Publishing Ltd., 2011.

Cook, Roger and Karl Zimmermann. *The Western Maryland Railway: Fireballs and Black Diamonds*, 2nd ed.. Laurys Station, PA: Garrigues House, 1992.

Fee, Elizabeth, Linda Shopes, Linda Zeidman, eds. *The Baltimore Book: New Views of Local History*. Philadelphia: Temple University Press, 1991.

Hahn, Thomas F. Swiftwater. *Towpath Guide to the Chesapeake & Ohio Canal: Georgetown Tidelock to Cumberland*, 15th ed. Harpers Ferry, WV: Harpers Ferry Historical Association, 1997.

Harwood, Herbert H. Jr. *Blue Ridge Trolley: The Hagerstown & Frederick Railway*. Huntington Beach, CA: Golden West Books, 1970.

High, Mike. *The C&O Canal Companion: A Journey through Potomac History*, 2nd ed. Baltimore: Johns Hopkins University Press, 2015.

Hill, Frederick B. *The Life of Kings: The Baltimore Sun and the Golden Age of the American Newspaper*. Lanham, MD: Rowman & Littlefield, 2016.

Hilton, George W. *American Narrow Gauge Railroads*. Stanford: Stanford University Press, 1990.

MacDonald, David and Priscilla Barrett. *Collins Field Guide: Mammals of Britain and Europe*. London: HarperCollins, 1993.

Mencken, H.L. *Newspaper Days: 1899-1906*. New York: Alfred A. Knopf, 1941.

Mitchell IV, Alexander D. *Baltimore: Then and Now*. San Diego: Thunder Bay Press, 2001.

Olson, Sherry H. *Baltimore: The Building of an American City.* Baltimore: Johns Hopkins University Press, 1997.

Page, Robin. *A Fox's Tale: The Secret Life of a Fox.* London: Hodder & Stoughton, 1986.

Petersen, Peter B. *The Great Baltimore Fire.* Baltimore: The Press at the Maryland Historical Society, 2004.

Rubin, Mary H. *Images of America: The Chesapeake and Ohio Canal.* Charleston, SC: Arcadia Publishing, 2003.

Schmidt, Alvin J. *Fraternal Organizations: "Knights of Pythias."* Westport, CT: Greenwood Press, 1980.

US Department of the Interior. *Chesapeake and Ohio Canal.* Washington, DC: National Park Service Division of Publications, 1991.

United States Postal Service. 2007. *The United States Postal Service: an American history, 1775-2006.* Washington, DC: Government Relations, US Postal Service, 2007. https://purl.fdlp.gov/GPO/LPS114451.

Williams, Harold A. *Baltimore Afire.* Baltimore: Remington Publishing, 1954.

Articles

Bruchey, Eleanor S. "The Development of Baltimore Business, 1880-1914." *Maryland Historical Magazine,* 64, no. 1 (Spring 1969): 18-42.

Calvert, Scott. "Mayor's Death, Blaze Still Linked in Mystery." *The Baltimore Sun,* February 7, 2004.

Cassie, Ron. "Then and Now: Public Markets." *Baltimore Magazine,* May 2014.

Coyle, Wilber F. "Robert M. McLane (1867-1904). In *The Mayors of Baltimore* (reprinted from *The Baltimore Municipal Journal,* 1919), 194-201. Maryland State Archives.

Girsdansky, Paul Scott. "The Decline and Fall of the Baltimore News American." College Park, MD: University of Maryland, 1989. https://drum.lib.umd.edu/handle/1903/20234

Millar, John D. "C&O Canal Boat Description." Hagerstown, MD: National Park Service, US Department of the Interior, 2018.

Schimf, John L. "I Remember ... Calvert Street Over 60 Years.: *Baltimore Sun,* September 9, 1956.

Siebert, Tom. "Secrets of the Belvedere." *Baltimore Magazine,* December 2003.

VanWestervelt, Rus. "Chasing Fire: Understanding the Death of Baltimore's Mayor in 1904." *The Baltimore Writer*, February 7, 2014, https://thebaltimorewriter.org/2016/02/07/chasing-fire-understanding-the-death-of-baltimores-mayor-in-1904/.

Watts, Marina. "'Unsolved Mysteries': A Brief But Morbid History of the Belvedere Hotel." *Newsweek*, July 6, 2020.

Websites

Aesop:

- https://www.litscape.com/indexes/Aesop/Titles.html
- https://interestingliterature.com/2018/08/a-summary-and-analysis-of-aesops-the-fox-and-the-grapes-fable/

C&O Canal:

- https://www.nps.gov/choh/learn/education/upload/A-Journey-on-the-C-O-Canal-oct-5-2011.pdf

Foxes:

- https://www.discoverwildlife.com/animal-facts/mammals/understand-fox-behaviour/
- https://www.nationalgeographic.com/animals/mammals/r/red-fox/

Mules:

- http://www.lovelongears.com/about_mules.html
- http://a-z-animals.com/animals/mule
- https://www.bensonranch.com/articles/stubborn-as-a-mule/

Newspapers:

- https://www.baltimoresun.com/about/bal-about-sun-sunhistory-htmlstory.html
- https://chroniclingamerica.loc.gov/lccn/sn90057201/ (The Herald)

Police:

- http://mdhistory.net/msa_sh248/msa_sh248_1/msa_sh248_1_1.pdf

Robert M. McLane:

- https://msa.maryland.gov/msa/speccol/sc3500/sc3520/012400/012492
  /html/msa12492.html

Trains:

- http://westernmarylandrhs.com

Western Maryland:

- http://www.whilbr.org/itemdetail.aspx?idEntry=1626&dtPointer=0
- http://www.ci.cumberland.md.us
- https://williamsportmd.gov
- https://www.hagerstownmd.org

Other Sources

- Maryland Center for History and Culture
- The historical archives of *The Baltimore Sun*
- C&O Canal National Historical Park, Western Maryland Railway Station, Cumberland, MD
- Association of American Railroads (2003), *Railroad Service in Maryland,* 2005.
- National Register Information System. National Register of Historic Places. National Park Service, accessed 2009.

TRIBE. LOYALTY. LOVE

JOHN THOMAS EVERETT

A tale of survival, adventure, and self-discovery.

www.braveshipbooks.com

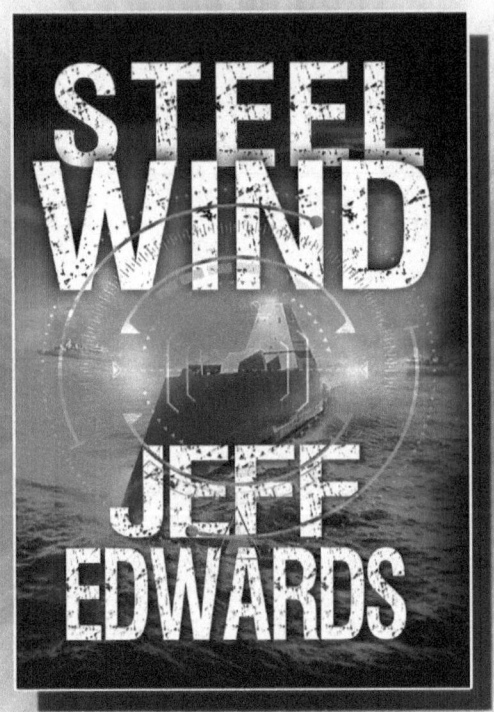

THE THOUSAND YEAR REICH MAY BE ONLY BEGINNING...

ALLAN LEVERONE

A Tracie Tanner Thriller

www.braveshipbooks.com